Penguin Fiction

I Know What I'm Doing

Hans Koning is now the pen name of Hans Koningsberger, who was born in Amsterdam, Holland. He studied at the University of Zurich, but he has been writing in English ever since serving in the British Army during the Second World War. Much of his life has been spent in travel, but since 1951 he has made his home in New York.

Four of his other novels, *An American Romance*, *A Walk With Love and Death*, *The Revolutionary* and *The Affair*, are also published in Penguins. He has also written *Love and Hate in China*, *Along the Roads of the New Russia*, *The Almost World* and the *Death of a Schoolboy*. His play, *Hermione*, was shown on the Continent in 1964, and he has written widely for newspapers and magazines including the *New Yorker*, the *New York Times*, the *Guardian* and *Punch*. He has also helped to write and produce films of some of his books.

Hans Koning

I Know What I'm Doing

Penguin Books

Penguin Books Ltd, Harmondsworth,
Middlesex, England
Penguin Books Australia Ltd, Ringwood,
Victoria, Australia

First published in the U.S.A. 1964
Published in Great Britain by André Deutsch Ltd 1966
Published in Penguin Books 1975

Made and printed in Great Britain by
C. Nicholls & Company Ltd
Set in Monotype Times

1

I was born in a dark, large house in Woldingham, which is twenty miles south of London. My father died when I was two years old, and my stepfather hated me, or so I have thought since my earliest memories. When I was sixteen, he arranged a job for me with an insurance company in London; he had told my mother and me that I was not the type of girl for a college education. The work meant getting up at six, six days a week, a freezing cold bathroom (both summer and winter, it seemed), and a slow train into town with compartments smelling like my stepfather's study where there was always a wet cigar butt in the ash tray.

It is strange for me to realize how little I remember of that time. When I think about it, I always see the same picture, of our dank and green garden which climbed a hillside, and of myself sitting on a bench near the upper road, reading; I read three or four books a week. When I was seventeen, my mother and stepfather went to the United States – he could not bear the Labour Party any longer, he informed my mother. He and I hardly exchanged a word in those days. My mother wasn't bothered by the idea of leaving me alone in England, and they never suggested I come with them. I moved to a rooming house in London, a dreary but respectable place, and made some new friends, girls whose dates were boys at the universities; and I didn't fit in too badly.

There was an autumn evening, about a year later. It was drizzling miserably as I came back from a dance. I stood in the doorway with the boy who had taken me there, and I had the sudden feeling that I could not go on with this kind of life one more day. I said good night and hastily went upstairs. A tepid smell came towards me as I opened the door: I had left my hot plate on. There was a knock; the man living on the floor above me said he had come to make sure the place wasn't on fire. I told him it was all right, but as he hesitated, I offered to make tea. His entrance had stopped me from crying, which I had been set on doing, and I felt grateful towards him for that. He had recently come out of the army and was now studying to be an engineer. I had gone to the movies with him once, but we hadn't exchanged more than a dozen words. When he had asked me out again, I had said I was busy.

This man stirred his cup as he sat in my overstuffed chair, and looked at me with sad dog eyes. My pleasure with his visit vanished. I thought, Why is this total stranger sitting in my room and putting his fleshy mouth to the rim of a cup of mine? I started to say, 'I'm very tired, you must go now,' but instead of that found myself saying, 'Don't look at me like that, please.' He put his cup down and blushed. 'Why do you?' I asked. 'Do you want to go to bed with me?' He stood up. I felt very strange; cold, and old. I reached past him and turned off the lamp. I stood up too, and then took all my clothes off and lay down on the couch. He stared at me and walked out of the room, and a great, warm feeling of relief came over me. Then I heard that he had not gone up to his floor but was in the toilet on my landing. He came back into the room, his face yellowish in the light from the street, and he took his clothes off. He was awkward and I looked away. He lay down on top of me, rather carefully, as if I were not a person but some sort of contour chair. He did not hurt me and then it was already over. He was my first man. I looked up at the ceiling on which vague rings of light were moving, and my thoughts wandered. I hardly knew where I was when he started speaking, quite unexpectedly and in a tone of voice I had not heard before. I didn't answer, and fell asleep; and when I woke up again he had gone. I slipped under the cover and felt pleased, simply to be alone in my bed which seemed very comfortable and secure just then.

2

I really do not know why I let myself drift from that evening on into an affair with my fellow boarder (his name was George). I didn't care: but I did mind that I didn't care. It lasted almost a year, and all that time he talked about our marriage and was certain we would get married, while I knew we would not. I cooked dinner for both of us almost every day, shopping after work – a nuisance since it was a struggle for me to get to the shops before they closed. George was home from his classes before me, but he never offered to do it, and I never suggested it. He didn't like going out to restaurants or to parties.

That winter a mid-term examination of his came up about which he had been brooding for months. I remember how strange and pale he looked on the evening of that day, sitting in my room when I came home. He had not gone to the exam, he told me, for he had been sure he would fail. He expected me to be angry or upset, but I only said, 'I guess you know best.' Two days earlier I had been to the American consulate during my lunch hour and filed a visa application for the United States.

I think now that my main reason for having George was that he kept me occupied. I didn't want the university crowd any more; they were certainly more amusing than George but they made me feel slightly uncomfortable. With George I was the stronger person. I did not want to be alone. Cooking, eating with George and then reading or going to a movie, suited me. I never thought of this life as the one I actually wanted to lead, and told myself I was passing time while waiting for it all to really begin. I was reading a different kind of books now, for I couldn't stand novels any more which treated things as so terribly important. Perhaps that was how I started thinking about going to America. I had got the idea that there my generation was very cool about life and love and all that. And I liked the space; England is so cramped.

I had been reading the newspapers, and seriously, since I was a girl in grade school; I stopped that when England started a war with Egypt to get back the Suez Canal. The things they printed then were too nauseating. Here it was the year 1956, with a two-year waiting list to get into a council flat or buy a Morris Minor, and then they had the nerve to dish out this reheated Kipling Save-the-Empire stuff.

At the end of our evenings, George always went back to his own room. He would say, 'Do you want to – ' or some such unfinished sentence, and if I didn't say no, he would make love to me. I can't say, 'We made love', for I didn't play much of a part in it. He was actually quite handsome and well built; I liked his physical presence except for his large hands and his skin which had that terrible London pallor. But I never looked at him when he was naked. I didn't like to be kissed on my mouth by him, nor have I ever liked that much from anyone. I also told him not to try to arouse me with caressing. I made him come into me carefully and then I functioned properly. He never asked me anything except, 'Should I wait?' and I always answered, 'No, please come now,' and sighed. But I was not moved by it at all.

3

I went to America in April, after a drawn-out disengagement from George. There were scenes and he forced me to make all sorts of promises – as if there were any value in promises made under pressure; as if one could promise to love somebody. I detest people shouting at me, and all it did was to make a total stranger out of him. Finally he clutched to the fiction that he would follow me later that year, as soon as he had passed his examination.

I didn't want him to come to Southampton; we said good-bye in Waterloo Station. I remember how I tried to look sad and how, as I leaned out of the compartment window of the boat train, there suddenly were tears in my eyes. George couldn't know this, but they were more for my sake than for his, for just then it seemed wrong to me, intolerable almost, that a whole year of my life could vanish into the past so tracelessly. As he let go of my hand, I was crying; I guess I was mourning the eighteenth year of my life, the one and only, lost now. Then I settled in my corner and took a deep breath. There was a girl sitting opposite me, who immediately started telling me about her ex-G.I. husband she was going to join in Toledo, Ohio, and soon we were in deep conversation.

4

The crossing of the ocean was different from what she had imagined it to be. Even before the ship sailed, the decks were emptied of people by curtains of icy rain sweeping in from the sea. The weather stayed raw the whole voyage, and the social life aboard was almost nil; there didn't seem to be anyone aboard she particularly wanted to talk to. The spectacle of the seasick middle-aged ladies hovering under blankets in their deck chairs, the jovial first-generation American businessmen with heavy accents, returning from a visit to the old country, filled her with dismay.

Three days out, the seas became so heavy that the ship had to heave to and lie still for several hours to avoid damage. It happened shortly before dawn; the sudden stillness awoke her. It was pitch-dark in the small inside cabin of which she was the sole occupant. She became aware of the rocking of the ship around her, of the metal smell in the air coming from the ventilator, just barely sickening. She felt with her hand along the ceiling of her bunk for the overhead light, but then she dropped her arm and lay still. She had the thought that the ship was in distress and that she was going to die. First she flushed hot and cold, but soon she became calm. She touched her small breasts, and her belly, through her nightgown, and pulled her legs up and let her hands glide down them to her feet. Then she hurriedly sat up and tucked the blanket back in again at her feet, and lay straight: there was a sense of security in that position. I have nice legs, she thought. Someone in the office had said a week before that she had the nicest legs in London. She conjured up an image of the sea closing over her. Are there waves under the surface? she wondered. She saw herself drift down through the water, the green massiveness of it surrounding her, stroking her legs. Somehow she fell asleep, and when she woke up again, the light was on, and the stewardess was standing in the cabin, saying with a little smile, 'Good morning, miss. I brought you some tea; it's a nasty day all right.'

5

But she seldom thought about death. When she was a child, she often went to church, on her own initiative. One day her mother, in a rare mood of worrying about her, realized she was away, found her there, and dragged her out in the middle of the service. She had cried for hours, and after that she had been free to go when she wanted to. She went for the mood of the place, especially for the music; when she was older, she loved hymn singing. The idea of God did not enter her mind; she did not remember ever having thought that death was not the end of everything and no one tried to tell her otherwise. The thought of the world without her made her dizzy, and she got over this by saying to herself, 'Well, that's the way the cookie crumbles.'

Her mother had never suggested that she should learn to swim, or to play tennis or to ride, and she had not become a particularly eager outdoors girl. She was tall, and when she was full-grown, at the age of seventeen, she had a grace of movement rather rare in a young girl. But there was also a physical timidity in the way she walked and moved, caused by a certain holding back within her, not by a lack of courage. She was never afraid as long as she could stay passive, in a fast car for instance; once an R.A.F. cadet took her up in a fighter plane and to his disappointment she was neither afraid nor thrilled. She had light-brown hair, dark eyes, and an oval face; sporadically she looked almost ugly, often very exciting and sometimes beautiful. She had an elegant, clear voice.

She was curious, not for knowledge but for emotions. She felt she should try to experience whatever there was – 'Try everything once,' a girl friend of hers, a divorcee at the age of twenty-one, had recommended as a motto, and she liked that. She wanted many things for herself from life, but she was never completely without awareness that it was all temporary, a short term, and that it did not really matter whether one lived to be twenty or seventy. This feeling was the main element in a great pride she had, a somewhat deadly pride. For although she was ready to use everybody to a degree, she felt that she needed nobody and would never at any future moment in her life be at another person's mercy – since it was easy enough to kill herself. Thus, since she had no pity for herself, she did not believe in having pity for anyone else either.

She had an aversion to most forms of snobbism, xenophobia, anti-Semitism, and political right-wingers, not because she felt sorry for the poor foreigners or Jews, but because she guessed the weakness hidden in those prejudices and hate feelings. She hated weakness, it embarrassed her.

She rarely thought of herself as belonging to 'modern youth', with all its problems that were constantly discussed in newspapers, movies, and theatre plays. When she was in company where the topic was brought up, she never participated. When she was asked her opinion on any abstract or general idea, she would answer with a joke. Thus she gave the impression of being a cheerful, rather superficial creature.

6

My last evening on the ship stands out for me, different from the earlier days smelling of seasickness. In a way the trip was over, but we hadn't arrived yet – we were suspended, sort of. At least that's what I thought that evening; perhaps it was just chance.

There had been a Captain's Dinner, distinguishing itself in Tourist Class only by a dessert of ice cream floating in some kind of flaming liquid, and ghastly little hats donned by all the fattest ladies and gentlemen in our dining room. I had got up as quickly as possible from our table, and as I wandered through the corridors, I came upon a crowd of young people I had not seen before. One boy put his arm around me, and I joined them. We hiked all over the ship, from the bakery to the bridge. The others were all slightly drunk, very gay, and they seemed appealing and wonderful. We laughed and shouted and sang songs. I felt more carefree than I'd ever been, nothing mattered – but in a nice way. We ended up on a deck in the crew's section where two sailors were playing on mouth organs. Even that music, which is terrible, seemed right. We danced. My young man, whose name I never learned, was an American college boy and a good dancer. We left the others, and ended up on a deck in the bow of the ship, in front of the bridge. There's no light there, so as not to hamper the lookouts, he explained to me. We sat on the deck, sheltered by some kind of metal box, and he put his arms around me and kissed me endlessly. We didn't do anything beyond that, but it felt warm and dear, and more exciting than George bashing away on me in bed. Then I got very chilled, and we started walking again. We found the others and finally everyone was exhausted and we all went off to bed, except for two girls who said they were going to stay up all night and wait for the first sight of America, which they had been told was the Ambrose Lightship.

When I woke up, I put on slacks and a sweater and went back out on deck. It was a grey, foggy morning with a drizzle. I was hung over, and leaned against the railing with my face tilted upward – the rain on it felt good. Suddenly a man beside me tapped me on the arm and pointed, without speaking. A dark line had become visible through the patches of fog – the coast of the United States. I swallowed, it was really quite moving. Then, precisely at that moment, I felt someone's mouth against my neck. I jumped, and turned; it was the boy of the night before. He started to say something, but when he saw how furious I was, he stopped. I thought he looked pale and silly and I wanted to be alone. Another man from the group came over to us, and as these two started talking, I said, 'Excuse me a minute,' and slipped away.

I found myself the most forward spot on the ship, and stayed there and stared at that coast, now visible, now veiled in shreds of fog, until the wind made my eyes water. I went to the dining room and ate a big breakfast, ignoring all the fuss around me about luggage, and passports, and the Statue of Liberty. When the immigration officers came aboard, I went past as one of the last of the passengers, fetched my overnight bag from my cabin, and walked off the ship.

7

I got settled quickly in New York. America has a different kind of problems, and things which take up most of your energy in England seem to get accomplished here almost unnoticed. I had had a choice of two jobs even before I left home, for British secretaries are in fashion, and I took the one at a large midtown office, which paid a hundred dollars a w ek. My main claim seemed to be my accent, but in the beginning I also worked much harder than the others, strictly from habit. I sat in a windowless room with one other girl, facing the door behind which our bosses were established. I had been told this was a glamorous job, but I was wise enough to know that was just nonsense. A job is a job, at least on my level; I don't like having to work for a living, but since I have to, I don't give it another thought. I didn't give a hoot about our glamorous clients because they didn't give a hoot about me; on the very rare occasions when one of them asked me a question in passing, he never focused on me but stared over my head, as if afraid I'd ask his signature or sue him or something. But later I found that other people were impressed with the idea that I had actually talked to some famous person.

I liked it that I didn't have to be in until after ten, and that you could stay away for an afternoon or even a day for vague reasons with no one questioning it; and I liked the neatness and shine of the surroundings, very different from the threadbare offices of London; it made me feel clean.

After a week at the Pickwick Arms Hotel I got a sublet on East 79th Street. It had a fireplace which excited all my visitors (not me, since I grew up in a house full of fireplaces which didn't stop us from freezing half the year); it took me very little time to take it all for granted and then get furious about something going wrong, like the bathroom door which used to get stuck.

My first friends were Jean, the girl in the office, a young man there who was a friend of hers and who took both of us to luncheon now and then, and a girl called Susan, the daughter of a textile manufacturer, who had been the only person to whom I had brought a letter of introduction from England. I was often alone on evenings and weekends but did not mind, for everything was so new, and I liked New York very much. Susan took me out of New York one of my first weekends, and drove the two of us all over New England.

I loved the landscape without end; those roads which are so long and straight that it makes you dizzy: it's like falling down to the horizon. And I loved the car radio. There's a sea of music covering the American landscape, with car radios like taps, drawing from it.

I talked to my mother on the telephone. She and my stepfather now lived in upstate New York. She had known, of course, that I was coming, but had not been at the boat. 'You must come soon for a weekend,' she said, 'as soon as you're free; you're probably quite busy with your friends – ' 'Yes, I am,' I had answered as pleasantly as I could. 'I'll let you know when I'm free.'

I had sent George a card, with the Statue of Liberty, when I had just arrived and was still at the Pickwick Arms Hotel, and they forwarded his letters to me: he sent two or three a week, using air letter forms. I glanced at them, I rarely felt up to reading them. It was always the same stuff anyway. But I never threw one away; I kept them in a drawer.

8

The girl beside me, Jean, was a tall, awkward creature with a nice sense of humour. She was from Stamford, Connecticut. She had bad teeth and always looked unwashed, and she had an apartment on Second Avenue which was large and dirty too. Her kind of humour, which tallied with that of many of the others at the office, was new to me; it wasn't what they called sick but it was based on the idea that most feelings are corny or phoney. I don't think those people were really that tough, though; I think they laughed together, and cried when they were home alone in bed.

Jean was a popular girl, with many friends taking her out, and quite chaste, as far as I could tell. She gave a party for me, and after that I got invitations too from these young men. I don't know why I wasn't more interested; I thought there was something tired and tiring about them.

With Susan I spent some Saturdays looking at apartments, for she had suggested that we should share one in the fall. One time we rang a bell at random in a building where we couldn't find the advertised place and came upon three young men sitting in a kitchen, drinking coffee. They asked us in. We all had a look at the apartment for rent and then the youngest, who lived on another floor, said he had to walk his dog. He was a heavy, crew-cut boy, who looked singularly placid. I walked with him. We went around the block a couple of times, talking about the usual things, how I liked New York and all that, and then we came back to his apartment to put his dog there. When we were inside the door, he started to kiss me. I didn't kiss him back, but I stood still, thinking foolishly, well, I should be able to say that I've had an American boy friend.

I think he was surprised when I let him undress me without

saying one word. I moved his hand away from me, but I stroked him, until he felt hard, and then I pulled him on me. It was indeed exciting, the idea, that is, of being made love to by an American. It put the seal on being there. There wasn't more to it than that, though.

I didn't go back to the others afterwards but went straight home. Susan never asked me why I had vanished, but she was obviously mad. The boy telephoned me a number of times, but I refused to have any more dates with him. He didn't understand; 'Do you have someone else?' he asked. 'I don't have someone else, and I don't have you,' I said.

9

There were Sunday mornings when she would wake up early and lie staring at the ceiling, not thinking very much, neither happy nor unhappy. The apartment windows faced north, and the blinds were down, but the shadows in the room and the filtered light showed when it was a bright morning. She would get up and make tea and toast for herself, and then creep back into bed with that, prop herself up and look through the Sunday *Times*, which was still being delivered for the lady whose apartment she had. Sometimes, she fell asleep again over the paper.

She would finally get dressed, in a blouse and slacks, and walk through Central Park. Or she would take the bus down Madison Avenue and ride forty or fifty blocks before she could bring herself to get off again. She didn't mind going back home with the sun still high: she liked to putter around in her apartment and to prepare her clothes for Monday morning.

It was a period such as she had not lived through before; she was completely free and abandoned at the same time. The quilt of weekend silence muffling the city, the sky a virginal early summer blue, the empty sunny streets; the long late evenings when the windows of the buildings across from her glittered in the red light of the sunset, and then turned grey and looked as void as if man had died out on earth – she felt anonymous in this setting, and unknown; unregistered, the opposite of England where all was described and circumscribed.

If it started to frighten her, this vacuum, she would just in time reduce it to its outward form. It was, after all, just a girl of nineteen waiting at a bus stop on a New York avenue, or looking out of her apartment window on an evening in June.

10

As I crossed the street one Friday after work with a bag of groceries, I just missed being run over by a convertible which had jumped the light. There were two boys and two girls in it; they stopped and looked back to see whether I was still on my feet. 'Watch it, you swine,' I shouted at them, quite unnecessarily, and that made them laugh like hyenas. They backed up and the driver said, 'I'm so sorry, ducks.' He was imitating my voice, but not maliciously, and I couldn't help smiling. He got out and pulled his seat forward. 'We'll give you a lift home,' he said. 'Perhaps she wants to come to the party,' the boy in the back said. 'That's a splendid idea,' the driver said, 'move over and make room for her, you swine.'

I rested my groceries on the trunk of the car and looked at them; none of them could have been older than sixteen.

It was a sultry day, with black clouds in the sky which glittered uneasily. The town already had the deserted look of a summer weekend. Jean had asked me to come out to Stamford the following morning, but only tentatively; she had said she had to check first whether there was room and then she'd call me.

'All right,' I said to no one in particular, and I squeezed into the back seat.

We picked up two more boys and then drove out onto Long Island. It was quite a way; the party, I was told, was in a beach house in Quogue, a two-hour drive. Once we were out of the heavy traffic, it was a lovely ride. It didn't rain, the heavy air rushed around our heads and made it impossible to talk, which was a great advantage. One of the boys passed a bottle of vodka around and I dug out a can of nuts from my grocery bag. The vodka was lukewarm and terrible, but I drank it, and when we got to the house, I was really drunk – the first time in my life, I think.

It was dark now. I walked down the steps to the beach and stood in the sand; the ocean was just barely visible with the surf gleaming; the wind was moist. Behind me were the lights of the house and the very loud music they were playing.

I took a deep breath, and climbed back up to the party. I felt very good. I danced, and drank a mixture of beer and vodka, and was kissed. At one point I was sick to my stomach, but I got over it. It all became a bit blurred, but I managed somehow, when it was already getting light, to find a room with a bed and a key in the door. I locked the door, put my clothes on a chair, and fell asleep like a stone.

11

There was no hang-over of any kind to that party. On Sunday evening someone gave me, and a couple, a lift back into town. Until then I lay on the beach, helped wash up, drank beer, and just sat around. No one questioned anyone else's reasons for doing or not doing anything. I was jealous of them; when I was their age, I worked and commuted, I couldn't drive a car, and I was ordered home by my mother at fixed hours (though she took no notice of what I did). These kids had a kind of sophistication that made me feel almost younger than they were. I had to fend off some of the boys and yet I felt I had to prove myself with them rather than the other way around.

It was a good weekend. On Monday morning I felt different towards Jean, who was annoyed that I hadn't been in when she did call from Stamford, and towards Farmer, the young man in our office: it was as if I had gained an advantage over them. I had come closer to the inside of things, to the core of the city, of America itself even. I was less impressed with their pronunciamentos on the facts of life and their jokes. Those Quogue kids had somehow known better what it was all about than Mr Farmer, junior executive of a large company. Perhaps it seemed that way, simply because they were ten years younger. Life in this country, I think, gets off to such a fast and magnificent start, and then it often peters out equally fast and is all over in a way by the age of twenty-five. It's like the Middle Ages. It's strange how it would be like that here of all places, with people so unmedieval in their comforts and philosophies, but it seems so to me. Or perhaps those teenagers had the edge on Mr Farmer precisely because they were not junior executives, because they were nothing, had nothing to lose, and didn't give a damn. That makes for sophistication.

After that weekend I began to accept dates, for now I could stand them better, those young men from I.B.M. and the advertising agencies. I still thought they were boring, but they couldn't perturb me any more; I observed them. I could sail beautifully through an evening, order myself a decent dinner, kid my escort a bit in the right way, laugh, see a movie or a play, and get back home hardly remembering the man's name or a word he had spoken. It was very pleasant.

12

But, suddenly, she became completely promiscuous. She did not know herself why. It wasn't that she was pushed into it by her way of life and her companions. Those men were slightly afraid of her, because she was cool and distant and ironic (and tall). She never brought any of them home; her apartment was inviolate to her, not her body. If a man seemed attractive as a man, and not unsympathetic, she would often accept the invitation to come for a drink in his place, to listen to his records, or whatever, and once there her escort would realize that she was willing. It might come as a bit of a shock to the man, or quite unexpectedly anyway; while he was fussing with glasses and ice and wondering what to do next, she'd settle down in a manner which seemed to say, well, you may prove yourself.

She was not trivial in her taste, she wasn't interested in handsomeness of the male-model kind. Manliness appealed to her, but it was a manliness of character or thinking, not of athletics. She began to be deeply intrigued with making love; more with the prelude, though, than with the act itself. Her excitement never carried her beyond a certain threshold. She never had an orgasm or any concentration of sensual feeling even, which could make her think it was one. The most exciting moment for her was seeing a naked man stand over her or lie beside her and see his sex become big and erect. She liked to stretch that moment and hold him off as long as possible. The idea that she caused that transformation was breath-taking for her, and she brooded about it while typing at her desk.

One evening she had gone to dinner with a date and to bed with him afterwards, and gone home early. As she stepped out of the taxi at her building, she saw someone waiting there for her. Oh my God, she thought, I forgot. She had had a date with that man too for the same evening, and it had slipped her mind. She couldn't help smiling; a pretty dashing situation, she thought. But then, when she saw that the young man was furious, she became furious herself for being waylaid like this. He immediately calmed down and asked her to come for just one drink in a bar near by; an hour later she was in his apartment and let him make love to her. Then she went home again; he wanted to escort her but she said no, she was all right.

She felt singularly pleased with herself as she got back into her apartment. She drew a bath and stayed in it for a long time, not in the least because she felt 'dirtied' but because she thought she owed the care to her body which had been used so much. She recalled the images of those two men at the height of their excitement, she looked down at her own body and thought, I did that, I have that power. She thought, I wish I could tell Jean, or someone, about tonight. (She never talked about sex, not even with a man she had made love with, and she hated dirty jokes.)

13

I had been told about the gynaecological clinic on 16th Street where one can go for birth control pills, and had got them for myself. I had known about them, of course, but never taken them.

They may not make much of a difference to this world getting more crowded by the minute, since so many people maintain that it is God's will that we multiply like rabbits; but I think those pills make very much of a difference to womankind. The mother of a friend of mine in London had been a suffragette, and what a dramatic thing that used to be! We were quite jealous in those days of that old lady and her cause – she must have had such a wonderful time getting all worked up about it, chaining herself to a lamp-post in front of the house of a cabinet minister, thinking she was doing something revolutionary. She wasn't, I don't think; we got the vote and nothing changed, everything stayed just the same rotten mess as before.

But the doctors who concocted those pills made a revolution, without anybody getting frantic or being chained to lamp-posts. It's simply the idea that you swallow a pill when you brush your teeth in the morning, and you're free – free for twenty-four hours, like a man, to do exactly what you want without any second thought. This seems real emancipation to me, and it is emancipation in our private lives, the only thing we have some control over, anyway. What happens in the world at large isn't really influenced by women voting nor by men voting; as Farmer always says when we talk about the heads of the firm, we're played for suckers anyway. I hope there were women among the doctors who created those pills.

14

I think I changed quite a lot during that summer, in things I did or didn't do, and also in the way I looked and dressed. I bought many new clothes and still managed to save some money. I got California cotton dresses, I threw out all my elaborate British underwear, and once I had some tan on my legs I even stopped wearing stockings. One day I had luncheon with a girl friend from London who was over for a visit, and found myself defending America, and sounding like an American down to my voice. She thought it was affectation, but it really happened by itself. I don't think, though, that my ideas about life changed; they're supposed to be fixed by the time you turn six years of age.

There were only a few of those murderously hot days I had been warned about, and I was happy in the city. Everybody who did leave town made so much fuss and complained so much about the traffic and the prices and the No Vacancies: they all seemed relieved to get back to New York. I was comfortable in my place and didn't mind in the least that I wasn't going anywhere – anyway, that's what I told people, and I think it was true.

In that period I became a very popular girl. A whole string of men were dating me and called me at all hours. Some were hard to shake off; in the office Jean answered the telephone and always waited for me to make some kind of signal. She could tell the most beautiful nonsense about my reasons for not being in. She was nice; we had fun about these men and she was certainly never envious. I had also lost interest in being chaste; when you make love, you don't have to talk, and it's less easy to get bored in general. Every real, final, intimacy with a stranger – and in the end that means with any man – gave me a tremendous kick. When you think about it afterwards, there's something so strange about it, unbelievable almost, that you'd let someone enter your body. If you didn't know others were doing it too, you'd feel it was madness.

And then, suddenly, it could seem stupid and even humdrum – and those two moods were just one second apart from each other; in me, anyway. But the first mood, about its being unbelievable, always came back, and then I felt I had to test it, and try.

15

Labor Day came up and they told us the office would be closed the Friday before. Everyone was excited except me who was secretly worried. Four days seemed a very long weekend to struggle through. I had refused an invitation from one man to come on a trip, which had seemed too much of a not very good thing. And then Jean told me she'd be off somewhere with her parents, and Susan was still away. So I told everyone I was finally going to visit my parents in Watertown, New York.

I called my mother, person-to-person, for I didn't particularly want to talk to my stepfather. She sounded happy to hear my voice, and I was pleased with my idea of calling. I told her I wanted to fly out on Friday, and would take a taxi to the house. 'Oh no,' she said, 'I'll come to pick you up at the airport.' But then, Thursday morning in the office, I got a call from her.

'I'm so sorry, dear,' she said, 'but would you mind terribly postponing your visit? Your stepfather has not been very well lately. He wants to use those days to get a real rest, and ...'

Jean was looking at me, so all I could answer was, 'Yes, sure, that's fine.'

'I'm very sad about this,' my mother said, and she did sound sad. 'I thought I might come to New York myself, one or two days in September, and we'll have a good talk.'

'Yes, I'd like that.' I said, 'Let's do that.'

And so, waking up on Friday morning in the silent house, I felt properly sorry for myself and had a good cry. I stayed in all day and didn't answer the telephone, which rang twice. I had some drinks all by myself, a spooky experience, and slept till one in the afternoon the following day. By four o'clock I really had to get out, and I walked to some terrible double feature on 86th Street. A man in the row behind me kept staring, but I didn't look back; when I came out of the movie house he was standing on the sidewalk. 'Please don't take this amiss,' he said, 'I'm simply a salesman from the Midwest alone in town, I just want a dinner companion.' I was foolish enough to stand still and listen, and he added, 'I know I annoyed you in there – but you have a wonderful face, I couldn't help looking at it.' I frowned and he started laughing. 'We have nothing to lose,' he said, and opened the door of a cab for me.

I probably went along because he didn't look like the kind of man you'd expect to accost somebody. He had a thin pale face and very light eyes, and seemed much too fragile to be interested in or capable of any nonsense. He took me to dinner in the restaurant of his hotel, a place on West 45th Street. It had a touch of decrepitness, but at least that section of town was less dead than my own was that Saturday. He did all the talking, about his travels, and the odd books he read, and after dinner he thanked me for listening. He said he was very broke, and would I come up with him to his room and drink some of the whisky he always carried with him. My mind was made up against him, but I came anyway; I wanted a drink, and I had never been afraid of any man.

16

That man, who had told me his name was Bill Daren, made me a bourbon and water and had me sit down with a book of architectural photographs; walked over and locked the door of his room, picked up an old-fashioned strap razor and slowly opened it. For a moment I thought this was a bad joke and then I became terribly afraid. There came a little smile on his face, which stayed and which was more frightening than the razor.

'If you do as I tell you,' he said, 'you'll walk out of here in a while just as you are now, and nobody will be any the wiser. If you don't or if you scream, I'll cut you up. It's all the same to me. Once I cut a girl's nose and ears off and I got quite a kick out of that. So what'll it be?' I don't remember answering anything, but I know I thought, It doesn't matter, I must do what he says. I'll just stop time.

I worked on him, I worked on his terrifying, thin, trembling body for what seemed a very long time, while he clutched the razor in his right hand and stared at me with the frozen smile. I did whatever he said.

Then he uttered a little scream, and lay still. I got hold of my dress and my pocketbook in one movement, unlocked the door and walked out; I did not look anywhere and I do not know whether he made an effort to stop me. I ran down that corridor naked and only at the elevator did I put on my dress. No one saw me. I had gone several blocks from the hotel before I realized that people stared at me and that my feet were bare.

When I got home, I put the dress in the fireplace, poured cleaning fluid over it and burned it. A stinging smoke filled the room for the flue was closed, but I liked that and inhaled it until I almost choked. Then I called the B.O.A.C. and booked a seat on a plane to London for the following day at noon.

17

I started packing frantically but after a while I slowed down. I had my hand on the telephone to call the police but didn't; it was too easy to imagine their faces and questions, even newspapermen perhaps, and later this man trying to get even with me. Those ideas of mine were based on how the papers here write about things.

I sat down on my bed and said, Pull yourself together. Wild and miserable thoughts whirled through my head.

If I live to be ninety, I thought, I can never be happy again. I'll never again let anyone touch me. I'll never have the courage to walk a New York street alone.

But all this ebbed away except for the feeling that it was impossible ever to be really carefree again. I called myself the worst names I could think of, and I staged some more of that ritual burning in the fireplace: two black lace panties I had bought a week before, and a dirty novel a boy friend had insisted on lending me.

I went to bed with the packing half-finished, and when I woke up, in the middle of the night, I called the airline and cancelled my reservation.

I made a mental list of things I'd henceforth do differently. I thought, I will comply, I'll never dare the world again. I won't so much as cross a street against the red light. I searched all over the apartment for something really abrasive, and finally I emptied my bottle of gin in the basin and washed my body with it. It stung badly. I drafted a letter to my mother, a sad one, then a bitter one, but didn't complete either.

I went back to bed with George's letters. They didn't make him feel dearer to me, as I had hoped they would. There was no sense of protection in them, they were too whiny. I fell asleep before I was through them all.

18

She entered a phase of punishing her body by being as spartan as she could bear, and went through a mania of cleanliness. She had a longing for purity but didn't know how to find expression for it. She walked into churches in her neighbourhood but got disconcerted by the jovial atmosphere, the American flag next to the altar, the ministers sounding like M.C.'s on television. 'Last week I read in a national news magazine . . . ,' one of them began a sermon, and she walked out and didn't try again. On a sombre day, with the first feeling of autumn, she took time off and went to Jones Beach by train and bus, and walked for an hour in the pouring rain. As she came back into the empty beach house, wet and shivering, with heavy sand in her shoes, and drank the terrible coffee from a paper cup, she felt more at peace than she had since that evening in the hotel room; she felt almost happy but didn't quite dare admit it to herself.

Then, the following morning in her office, she looked through a woman's magazine and came upon an article on venereal disease. A shiver ran down her back; the sudden and absolute certainty that she had been infected in the hotel hit her like a blow. She turned so pale that Jean noticed it. 'I don't feel well,' she said, 'I have to go home.'

Downstairs, she went into the drugstore next to her building and with trembling hands looked up the list of physicians in the telephone directory. When she had found one near by who would see her immediately, she took a taxi over. 'I'll soon know,' she told herself in the waiting room, 'this is the worst moment.' But the doctor, who was almost disappointingly cool about her visit, informed her that she had to await the results of two tests.

'Call me next Monday,' he said.

'Won't you know before?' she asked.

'I may have the results Friday afternoon,' he answered. 'If you want to try.'

She had given a false name and address, and paid immediately.

Three days – each day she went directly home from her office, in great haste to be alone and isolated. She had put her telephone in a closet, buried under a blanket to muffle the ring. Two or three times during the evening she would jump up and study herself in the bathroom mirror, looking for a rash or some other sign of corruption. Thursday, which she called afterwards for herself, 'my fear day', she felt frozen, she did her work with mechanical little movements. She visualized herself dead, her body putrefying in the earth. It seemed to her as if she could feel a process of putrefaction having started already inside her, of little worms nesting in her belly. Several times she left her desk, fearing that she had to vomit.

On Friday she forced herself to wait with her call, first until two, then until three in the afternoon. Finally, she dialled the number which she knew by heart and asked for the doctor. When she gave the name she had used on her visit, the nurse said, 'Oh yes, madam, your tests are here, they're all negative.' 'Oh,' she stammered, 'you mean positive? you mean I'm all right – .' I've been luckier than I deserved, she thought. She took a deep breath, and felt a wave of warmth flow through her and make her blush darkly.

19

Soon enough I recovered from all this. I don't quite know how and why, but I suppose people always do. It's comforting but I resent it almost, that nothing lasts, not even misery. My sublet ended and I took an apartment with Susan on East End Avenue, in a run-down block in the middle of a good neighbourhood, and we paid only thirty-seven fifty a month rent, without a lease because it was to be torn down soon. It was a railroad apartment and I had the front room. Susan had a habit of leaving the door open when she went to the bathroom, and right under my window were what seemed about a hundred garbage cans, but apart from those drawbacks it was a splendid find. Susan and I got along very well; when I set my mind to it I can get on with almost everybody. I made my own room liveable with little trouble, and liked staying home now evenings, reading; it was a pleasant way of being alone, for Susan would come in some time around eleven or so and talk to me awhile, or bring a boy friend for a drink. If I was in bed with the light out, she would just tiptoe through to her own room, but she'd always wake me for she was a well-meaning but clumsy girl.

My mother's visit to New York came off with a touch of comedy. On the plane from Watertown she had met a neighbour who was going to New York for shopping and the two ladies decided to share a hotel room in the Croydon. Thus, when I went up there after work, I got a really noble welcome from my mother who was very happy to see me, and proud of me, and who laughed with Mrs whatever-her-name-was about the independence of the new generation: here was this daughter of hers, already half a year in the U.S. and this was the first time they got together, and when she, my mother, was nineteen she had never been away from home, and all that stuff. And then my mother put her hat back on and we went down together, and she led the way into the hotel restaurant which looks more like a coffee shop; and we sat down; and she opened her mouth, thought, and closed it again. She had nothing to say to me and nothing to ask.

I could have become morose but instead I gave her a menu and picked one up myself and said heartily, 'Let's have a drink first, mother.' I saw her look at the menu with just a barely noticeable flutter (the place was quite expensive for what it was) – that is to say, a flutter she meant me to notice. Or perhaps I was just imagining it. Anyway, it made me add, 'And you're my guest.'

'Oh no,' she said.

'I insist,' I said. 'It's my town here now. And you were sweet to come down just to see me.'

She smiled, quite pleased. 'George *was* put off,' she said. 'I never leave him alone, he hates eating in restaurants.'

That was of course not my ex-George (who hated eating in restaurants too), but my stepfather whose name is also George. Without really saying the words, I answered for my own satisfaction, Why the poor bastard, I hope he chokes on it. And nuts to you too, you stingy bitch.

20

Fall came and it was a quiet life. One by one, all those boy friends stopped calling because whatever they suggested, I always said I was busy. Each of them thought that someone else had become my full-time date. A few still asked me to their parties and to these I'd go, dragging along Susan; when they questioned me, I smiled mysteriously, and they'd laugh and say I was a bad girl, and I'd laugh back. I enjoyed that.

But it was all in all lonely, and on weekends not too easy. I found that it made a big difference that I hadn't gone to school in this country and had no friends around from that period to fall back upon; perhaps school friends are the only ones who really stick with you. Those years you share are different from any later years. (I would hate to become a nostalgic looker-back at this early age; I used to look ahead so completely that my past didn't exist.)

As we all read in the magazines, life in this country is organized in a pattern of couples, not just for older people as in Europe, but from the age of ten on, I think. I like eating out and going to movies, but none of that I could do alone; even the movie previews for which we got tickets at the office were tricky. Everybody always stared and sort of pitied me, thinking I couldn't find a boy to take me. It had surely been a lot simpler during the summer when I was at all the movies on opening night and in the restaurants and night clubs and hopped into bed with my escorts afterwards. It sounds paradoxical, but I was in a stage of innocence then, I could never go back to that.

The city was wonderful those months of September and October. I'd walk down Fifth Avenue after six from my office and look in the shiny windows. It was dusk, the lights went on high up in the buildings and made the air seem deep, dark blue;

there was something about that contrast of the lights and the blueness, that made me unspeakably nostalgic.

Not for home, not for any place, but for a time going by unused.

On Sundays I took the habit of walking over to the boathouse in the park with my paper. The boats were already laid up, and I just sat and stared at the ruffles the wind blew over the water of the pond. There was never a soul there early in the morning except one queer-looking young man who seemed to spend his days staring at the sun with a tin-foil reflector around his neck. The sun was just comfortable; the air was so clear that I imagined I could smell its pureness; the world was very clean.

21

And then it started to rain and rain. Susan and I ran off to work mornings wrapped in various cellophane outer garments and huddled at the stop under her umbrella waiting for a crosstown bus – without fail one drove off as we rounded the corner. We swore the driver waited till he saw us and then closed his door.

When I came out at six it still rained, the asphalt shone, the avenue was choked with cars blowing their horns at each other.

It was in that period that I began going out with the client. Jean and I called him that when he first started telephoning, and the name stuck in my mind, changing from an ironic to a friendly label. He was a client of the firm of course, and fifteen years older than I. He was tall, thin, and quite striking. Jean said he looked like an American Albert Camus. He came in one morning at eleven when our two bosses were both in meetings and Farmer introduced him to us and we sat around for ten minutes and had coffee from the cart. He was amusing. I saw him several times after that and he always greeted me warmly but never said more, which was slightly disappointing. One day we came out together at midday and stood in the doorway peering at the grey sky and he took me to luncheon in a place near by. He asked me about my own life and talked about his work; about himself he said only that he was married, and that he had planned to ask me to lunch and had just been biding his time. I told Jean later I liked him and she groaned. 'Please don't start an affair with a married man,' she said. 'Not you too. Why? There must be some non-queer bachelors left in this town.' I agreed that it would be a bore and promised to be wiser than that. The following day he phoned and that was when Jean, covering the mouthpiece, first said, 'Here's the client for you – ' pronouncing the word with a hoarse Brooklyn accent, something like 'claar-yunt', at which we both started laughing crazily. I didn't want to keep the man dangling and motioned to her to think up an excuse, but she just put the receiver down on her desk, and I finally picked it up and agreed to a dinner date with him. After that, we had lunch or dinner once or twice a week. For dinner he always took me to out-of-the-way places, because – so I realized after a while – he couldn't be seen with me by his friends. I didn't mind. I liked him, and at times, driving somewhere with him in a taxi, I thought I actually desired him – a feeling I had never independently produced for any man.

22

She was not given to investigations of her own purposes and motives. She was often asked the usual questions about how she felt in New York, and whether she ever longed for England: her immediate answer to that always was, 'Oh God no. Never.' Thus she had slowly discovered, listening to her own answers, that she meant it. She liked playing up her Britishness a bit; it seemed a social plus in America and she enjoyed being teased about her accent, about the Queen, and all that. But except for her hour of panic after the hotel adventure, she had not ever considered going back.

She felt without analysing it that the values of the world around her suited her totally.

Once a young man had told her over dinner that the promise of 'the pursuit of happiness' was not a Fourth of July phrase but had been realized.

It meant, he had informed her, that everyone had the right to make himself as pleasant a life as possible. She remembered that conversation clearly. She had answered that it was just the same in England; but she knew in her heart that it wasn't so, although she could not quite see where the difference lay. There was more of an idea of *service* in England, which was precisely what had made her uneasy there. She had never made up her mind whether it was hypocrisy, a trick to keep the lower classes at it, or almost as bad, whether it was real and meant committing yourself to a society, an old society she wanted no part of.

She felt vague about the idea of marriage but since she did not want to become a career woman, she knew she should get married. She knew she could be a good housewife and would enjoy that role. There was something disconcerting, obviously, about being tied down and having one's life determined to such a large degree. Love should make that palatable, but she did not quite believe in love although she would not have admitted it to herself.

Picking a man was picking a way of life, an atmosphere, a group of friends and acquaintances, and it was no irrevocable choice. She knew she was desirable. She took good care of her body and always would. She could cook, and get along with people. A man who would get all that, and provide her with a home base in return, support her and travel around with her, would get his money's worth.

23

On my birthday (30 November, I was born under the sign of Sagittarius), the client sent roses to the office in the morning, three dozen, which impressed the girls no end, and late in the afternoon he showed up himself. He said he had come to see about some mail, but then he sat down on a corner of my desk – which seemed out of character – and told me he had a car downstairs and was taking me to dinner in the country. 'I can't,' I said, for Susan, with an enormous display of measuring cups, cook books and ingredients, had been baking a birthday cake for me. 'I insist,' he said.

'I'd have to go home and change first,' I told him.

'I'll wait for you in the car.'

We drove up into Westchester in the dark evening and I stared out at the dripping trees and the glistening lawns. We didn't speak much; mostly the only sounds were of the tyres against the wet road and the swishing of the windshield wipers. We had our dinner in a restaurant over a little stream; the food was bad but there was an open fire which was cheerful. We got back into the car and drove off; after a while I asked, 'Aren't you going in the wrong direction?' He actually blushed and looked at me without answering. I thought for a moment, and then I touched his hand with mine.

When he pulled into a motel, I waited in the car until our room had been opened and the manager had gone back into his office. Then I walked in and sat down, without taking off my coat; he bent over me to kiss me on my mouth but I closed my lips tightly and rolled my head away. He smiled, sat down on the floor, pulled my pantie girdle down my legs, and started kissing my belly. No one had ever done that to me before, and it was rather odd to say the least, particularly since we both still had our coats on. Heaven knows, perhaps that's why I didn't object. I just leaned back in my chair, and I liked it.

He went on with this for a long time, and I began to ache inside, a strange dull pain, like a headache almost in my belly. I leaned forward and tried to undo his belt, and then we both stood up and undressed hastily. It was a wonderful feeling when he came into me, a very great relief. It was a sensation impossible to put down in words, a bit like the feeling of water going down your throat when you've been absolutely parched. He got me very excited, and when he asked, 'Can you?' I said loudly, 'No, not yet,' for I didn't want it to end suddenly. He lay still, and then started moving again wildly, and I liked all of it, the feeling and the sight. He had a nice body. My excitement became a general feeling of happiness, physical happiness I guess. I wanted to feel him come now, and put my hands on his hips and pushed him in and out as hard as I could. I slipped my hand under my body and stroked him. He couldn't resist that.

In the car he said, 'I know it's ungentlemanly to ask, but how old are you today?'

I didn't answer and then we grinned at each other. 'I know I'm too old for you,' I said.

Susan was waiting up for me in the kitchen with her cake, with twenty candles on it. It was so sweet of her, I almost cried.

24

She lay awake for a long time that night. It was raining hard now and the drops pelting on the ash cans outside her window made a curtain of sound for her.

For the first time in her life, she was obsessed with the mystery of sex, the mystery of difference.

The painful emptiness in a girl, waiting to be filled, extended, by a man's sex – What a splendid arrangement of God, or nature, she thought. There is nothing accidental or trivial about it, nothing banal or unaesthetic. It's the most *sensible* thing in the world. A man seemed the most appealing subject in creation to her then. She was not thinking about herself now, about the power stored in being wanted. She was thinking of her man of that evening, 'the client', as an isolated person, a complete object. She contemplated him and admired him for being a man in the most narrow biological sense of the word, for not having a hollow, or being neutral – she imagined a neutral being with a smooth belly, like a doll – but for sticking out. It is excess matter, she thought, not necessary for surviving, a luxury, like all good things.

She pursued those thoughts and the man became a thing almost, a statue. She brought herself back into the image, but in an active way. That was what was new. She had always been outside what really happened in bed, her body a means to power in a way she accepted but did not even quite understand. Now she suddenly looked at this man as an instrument of pleasure. She thought of how she had moved him with her hands as if his body, all of him, was simply a handle for her use, a handle to move his sex with. Feeling that pleasure is enough of a justification for having a body, she thought. It's not necessary to use one's body for extraneous ends. It's enough to receive those waves of sensation with it, like a radio receiver – or almost enough.

Perhaps all this is just my way of saying that I love the man, she then suddenly told herself. Love. If he were castrated tomorrow, I'd never want to see him again. Can love be narrow, focused on one place? Geographic love, she thought. She shook her head, rubbing the back of it against her pillow. She said half-aloud, 'I'm twenty, a third of my life is over.'

25

I was up again before eight the following morning and had time for breakfast which rarely happened on a working day; then I walked to my office, I felt so marvellous. I was the first person there, and cleaned up my own and Jean's desks. I decided not to say anything to her – when he calls, Jean will guess anyway, I thought. However, he did not call that day.

By five o'clock I was miserable because there was only one hour left in which he might telephone, but then I shrugged it off. I called Susan at her office and we made a date to go to a movie together after work. And I never gave it another thought for the rest of that day. To hell with him.

The mail delivery in our street is quite early and when I rushed out of the house the following morning, back in the habit of being late, there was a letter from him. I read it on the bus. It was a good letter. Too good, possibly: when I read Jean some sentences from it, she swore she had heard those precise words in an old John Gilbert movie. I said she couldn't have, for John Gilbert had only been in silent movies. Still, I liked the letter. He announced among other things that it had been the most wonderful evening in his life. He also said that he was dreaming of my sloping shoulders which were out of a Sir Joshua Reynolds painting, and of my long legs, and of various other parts of me he listed, and that I had crept under his skin. He was terribly sorry that he had to be away for some days, and he counted on seeing me the moment he came back. 'I love you, I think,' he ended.

I dreamt that night that I was riding a scooter with George, sitting behind him and holding my arms around him very tightly. It wasn't raining but the asphalt was gleaming wet. It was twilight. The street was empty. I saw we were on Fifth Avenue; he has come to New York then, I thought, feeling neither pleased nor sorry with that discovery. From far off, I saw a traffic light, which was the only light in the dark street. It was green, but George slowed down. He knows it will turn red before we get there, I thought. But the light stayed green and he accelerated again. It took us a long time to get to it, and just then it changed to red, a bright red reflecting in the asphalt. George braked sharply. The scooter spun around and I dug my hands into his sides, but I fell off. I found myself landing very softly on the sidewalk and as I sat on its edge, I saw George somersaulting through the air and coming down headfirst on the pavement with a sickening crack. He's dead, I thought. Then I woke up; and I suddenly realized that his letters had stopped, quite a while ago actually.

Later I found out why. My mother telephoned; I must have sounded surprised for she quickly said, 'I'm calling because a boy friend of yours in England is writing me frantic notes.' 'What?' I said. 'He, his name is George, says you've left the Pickwick Hotel' – my mother pronounced that name fastidiously, as if she visualized dirty bedclothes and stained carpets –'without forwarding address.'

What had happened was that the hotel had stopped sending his letters on to me but had returned them to him. 'He wants me to make you write,' my mother said. 'He says it doesn't matter what; he just wants to know.'

'All right,' I said lamely.

'Well please do,' my mother asked. 'He scares me a bit, he sounds a bit wild. And,' she then added, 'would you like to spend Christmas up here with us?'

'Well, yes,' I said.

26

The client reappeared. It was a new experience to me; I had never known a man intimately whom I respected and who knew more than I. He was a serious man, too serious for me in a way, but he had a sense of humour, my kind of humour, all the same. He talked about politics too much, that is to say, he 'bothered', and he didn't understand that I did not refuse to read the newspapers from self-centredness, but because I didn't want to waste any more emotion on that phoney boloney, all those elder statesmen with one foot in the grave and one in their mouths. Heaven knows I'm not an Angry Young Woman, nor was I in London when it was quite the thing; but I can see I'd become one if I followed *them* from day to day. I don't even want to talk about it. I didn't particularly delight in being taken by him to meetings and forums where they always have a movie with the projector breaking down; I did enjoy United Nations receptions and things like that. He was an elegant man with an air of being above it all, and that's how he carried it off. I loved the feeling of being with somebody who was somebody, whom people recognized.

I don't know why he was in that period less concerned with gossip about us. Perhaps his wife was abroad; I never asked anything about her and he never mentioned her. Perhaps he really got carried away with himself over me. He told me he was in love with me, and he sent me picture postcards with the Statue of Liberty to my office with that message. It was nice to hear, and I often asked him, 'Who do you love?' 'Only you,' he would answer. Or when he was annoyed with me, he would just say, 'It's *whom.*' My geographical love, of that first evening in the motel, stayed as strong or even stronger, and I told him that he had a wonderful body and why. I liked touching him. But I never said to him that I loved him.

I caught a wicked cold then. After four days of it he convinced me to tell them at the office that I had flu and needed a few days off to sit in the sun somewhere. I didn't want to ask, but he pushed me into it and then I was glad I had done it, for they so readily said, 'Well, yes, of course,' that I called myself a fool for all my scruples. And that very afternoon he showed up at my apartment in a car he had rented, and we drove off to Miami.

27

I don't think I've ever been as happy as that dark winter afternoon sitting beside him and driving down the New Jersey Turnpike. I had just five free days ahead of me but I had a feeling of a vast expanse of time. There's a sense of excitement about travelling, which now combined with that warm car in the bleak landscape, the idea of going towards the sun, of waking up tomorrow – a day in the middle of the week – with no work to go to and nothing to do and with him to be responsible. It was about true what I had told at the office, I did have a semi-flu; and after our dinner I wrapped myself in a blanket and slept in the front seat. I would wake up at times from our car slowing down at a light or behind a truck, I'd peer at the oncoming headlights which silhouetted the two of us for one moment, smile at him, and go back to sleep.

Before noon the following day we got on a long ferry ride in Virginia, and on the southern shore of the water the bleakness of the weather had gone, it was spring there with patches of light blue in the sky. I threw my blanket and scarf in the back seat and decided that my cold was over. I was at perfect peace with him, with the world, and with myself. The roads became empty, and he let me drive the car most of the afternoon.

The third day we came before dark to a hotel on Sea Island which is just north of the Florida border, and we both said at the same time that we didn't want to drive any more that day. We had a splendid room. He went off to swim, but that was a bit too much for me and I had a hot bath instead. When he came back into the room he got into my bath with me, which took me somewhat aback. 'I know it's corny,' he said, 'but I like it.' I muttered that I didn't think it corny at all. We dried each other off, and stood beside each other in front of the long bedroom mirror. He became shy and stood behind me, but I pulled him back. We looked splendid together. He brought a chair and sat in front of the mirror, and made me sit on him with my face towards the mirror. I could see his sex entering me, I touched him, it was like touching part of my own body, as if I were a man; it made me dizzy. We lay on the bed and I made love differently from ever before. I wanted to try everything and wanted him to do everything. I was without any inhibition and without any complex idea about shame or morals or even love; I just felt my body sharply, every square inch of it, and wanted to be given every conceivable sensual pleasure.

He asked me at one point had I come, and I answered that I did not know and that he must never ask me that. We had dinner in the hotel, and we danced. He was a bad dancer, but I didn't mind in the least.

28

On Saturday things weren't quite as rosy as before. He was quiet, and the traffic along Route One down to Miami was very bad. I asked him whether he was all right and he said he was fine and just tired of driving. I played the car radio and fed him Cadbury chocolate bars and sticks of chewing gum. It was late when we got into the town of Miami, and we had both fallen completely silent. At that point we had a flat tyre. He climbed out of the car to look at it, and then he just stood there, while I sat in my seat and smiled at him. But he suddenly opened the door on my side, and shouted at me, 'For God's sake, do I have to do everything, can't you get out and help? Or are you too tired from doing nothing?'

It was no great drama, but it produced a change. A minute before I would have been unable to visualize him shouting at me; a minute later I was equally unable to visualize him as a man who could never shout at me. Soon enough I forgot the whole business; perhaps there was even some relief in that he was not perfect. He apologized later.

We had an inedible dinner and then he drove around on the lookout for a sidewalk café. He said the one thing he needed now was to lounge for an hour on a café terrace under the open sky. However, we didn't find any; the town believes more in air conditioning. He described the Paris sidewalk cafés to me and asked whether I would spend a vacation in Europe with him. I said yes. We took a room in a small hotel, made love and went to sleep. The following morning we crossed the boulevard and lay in the sun on the municipal beach, and I even let myself be convinced to have a swim. Swimming in December was still a wild idea. And then we took the car back to the rental people and flew home to New York.

He dropped me at my apartment and kept the taxi. We kissed, and I said, 'Thank you very much. It was wonderful.'

He smiled and said, 'You're very welcome. I thank *you*. And I do apologize for shouting at you.'

'That's quite all right,' I answered. He waved, and he climbed back into his cab and drove off. I went inside. Susan was fast asleep. I had a look at my face in the bathroom mirror. I was sunburned. Not bad, I thought, not half-bad.

29

It was nice to get back to the office and be told how great I looked. And then he started telephoning me. First he called to say good morning, and what a splendid time he'd had, and what a wonderful girl I was, and finally that he wasn't free that evening. That was fine with me, I wanted some time to myself to do my washing and things, but an hour later he called again and said he just wanted to make sure I wasn't mad at him, and it was a business appointment and on and on – a bit silly, actually; and it was hard to get him off the phone. And at five he called once more to make sure that I'd be free and see him the following day. 'What have you done to this poor man?' Jean asked. I grinned at her. 'She's llovely, she uses Pond's cream,' Jean said to Farmer, making very thick L's.

Susan had gone home to her parents for two days, so I invited the client to our railroad apartment and cooked dinner for us. I enjoyed that, cooking for someone again. I made a beautiful fish and custard with strawberries in it, and he was impressed.

After that, he wandered out of the kitchen and to my room, pulling me along. I told him Susan might come home that evening. 'I'll hide under the bed,' he said, but I didn't feel too good about it. I put the chain on the door and sat down. He looked at me, stood up, and took his clothes off, which decided the question. Usually women undress first. It is interesting to sit neatly dressed in a chair and have a naked man in your room.

After he had made love to me, we lay silently on my bed. I had turned off the light and pulled up the venetian blinds. A diffused light filled the room. We were stroking each other very lightly, just with one finger. Then I put my mouth near his ear and said in a low voice, 'I love you too.' He did not answer and kissed me on my mouth.

I laid my head on his shoulder, and we both fell asleep. I woke up because he put my head on the pillow.

'I'm sorry, dear, I have to go,' he said.

'What time is it?'

'I don't know, about eleven.'

'Only eleven?' I asked. 'Stay awhile longer.'

'No, I'd better not. I'd fall asleep again. I have so much work to do still. You go back to sleep.'

Once he had closed the front door behind him, I felt wide awake. The bed was clammy. I got up, put on a bathrobe, and started to clean the kitchen. Then I made myself a cup of hot chocolate, changed the sheets, and went back to sleep.

30

We established a routine, I cooked dinner for him once or twice a week and he took me out on one or two other evenings. In my apartment we had to time ourselves on Susan, and if I knew she might come home early, we'd make love before we had dinner, with the chain on the door. It wasn't too satisfactory. He lived on Long Island but he had a small place in town, more an office than an apartment, and I didn't like being there. It was too uncomfortable, the bathroom wasn't clean, and I hated undressing and then later getting into the same clothes again and going home. Once he just stayed in bed and let me wander off, but though I didn't say a word about it, I broke our dates for the following two evenings. After that, he always took me home, or, if he was very tired, I let him put me in a taxi. His place was just one room with a kitchenette in it, and a bathroom, and the only furniture was a desk, some chairs, and a bed. The telephone was right beside the bed and when we came in, the first thing he would do was to turn the sound down. But you could still just barely hear the ring, and he never answered it. At times it seemed to ring endlessly and it was maddening that he refused to pick it up. Once it started ringing while we were making love and he was in me, and when he wouldn't take the call, I pushed him off me and got dressed. I always went home early if we were at his place. 'Can't you sit quietly with me and read?' he asked, but I had nothing to do there. I needed my own things around me, to make myself comfortable.

I took up dating boys again, only because I didn't like sitting home evenings, wondering whether he would call, but I never made a date if he was free, and I never even kissed anyone else. It would happen that he called at the last moment to say that he was free after all, and then he acted terrible if I refused to break my date, and he'd call Susan at all hours to check on the time I was getting home. One evening I offered to come by his place first, and when I got there I found him sulking at his desk. 'Crosspatch, lift the latch, sit by the fire and spin,' I said.

He laughed halfheartedly.

'Well,' I said, 'quick, make love to me.'

'Are you sure you wouldn't rather keep it for your next appointment of the evening?' he asked.

I walked out, but he ran after me and said he was terribly sorry, and we kissed and I said I accepted his apology. We made love beautifully, and I was very tired in the theatre where my poor real date of the evening took me. In the intermission I suddenly thought I saw him, with a woman, standing near the door. I was horrified and half hid behind my escort until I saw I had been mistaken. Since then I was often concerned about meeting him with his wife somewhere, and I resented that, for it made me nervous about being in places I enjoyed.

31

On Christmas Eve I flew to Watertown to visit my parents. The client was with his family; the day before we had had dinner and he had given me my present; he had also told me after much hesitation that he had a daughter. I had said I liked him for that, I liked the idea of him having fathered a child. I was carrying a Christmas present for my parents, something unusual in our relationship; it had been hard to choose for they weren't much interested in anything, I don't think. I finally bought them a little English water colour in a frame.

It was my first American Christmas and the bustle excited me. In New York it rained, but when we landed at Syracuse I stepped out into a clear freezing night, with a touch of snow on the ground, just enough to shimmer in the half-light. Throngs of people were milling around in the airport terminal, the place was decorated – terribly, with blinking little lights and artificial holly, but festive all the same – in the restaurant they had piped-in carols and 'White Christmas', and, cutting through it all, the voice over the amplifiers was calling the beautiful names of unknown towns, Montreal, Montpelier, Indianapolis, and even San Francisco. There were many pretty girls, in fur hats, travelling in twos and threes, and young soldiers and air force men or whatever they were (I don't like men in uniform), and everyone looked sleek and organized and was toting expensive pieces of luggage. A great wave of restlessness rolled over me in that airport.

Then we were off in another plane, and at Watertown I found my mother sitting in her car outside the little wooden passenger building. She leaned out of the window at the curbside and cried, 'Hello there! Merry Christmas.' It was a warm welcome and as we drove off together she offered me her cheek and said, 'Give us a kiss.' The ride wound through dark lanes, past houses squatting behind Santa Clauses and sleighs and Christmas trees hung with coloured lights, until my mother suddenly performed an unorthodox turn into a driveway and came to a stop; 'Here we live,' she said. I put my overnight bag in the hall at the foot of the staircase and sat down with her in the living room. They had a Christmas tree. My mother looked very thin, but I told her she looked well. Then her husband came in and shook hands with me and offered to make us a drink, all very jolly.

That night I lay in a small neat bed, thinking hard. I had a very comfortable room, with a white rug and pink curtains, solid and with that countryside cleanliness no place in the city can ever achieve. On the night table an alabaster angel held a lamp, and in the drawer was a bright-yellow Jefferson County telephone directory and an anthology of condensed novels. My mother had turned the cover for me, and that, and the matching pillowcase with its little edges, the total darkness in the room once I had turned off the lamp, and then my mother's voice for a moment in the corridor, too soft for me to distinguish the words, it all made me feel as if I were a child again. And suddenly and quietly I burst into tears; suddenly it seemed unbearable to be twenty, to be growing up and growing old, and to die; to carry alone that terrible responsibility of struggling through life. I thought of the client and I hardly recognized myself in the girl who so happily made love to him and didn't give a damn that he was married and not really even available, the girl who was so above it all. And then I thought of young people, of those self-possessed girls at the Syracuse airport travelling all over the place, of the Quogue kids and that beach party, and I calmed down. I am also very young, I told myself. I'll find a berth.

It was an easy weekend, they were pleasant towards me and towards each other. We didn't talk much but read papers and magazines and watched television. One morning my mother and I went into town to shop, and she bought me a pair of very good suede gloves. She gave me those letters George had written her, but didn't ask me anything, which was a relief. And then the time was up, I thanked my stepfather for his hospitality, and she drove me back to the airport. We were late because we had waited for her husband who originally had said he wanted to do the driving, and she kept muttering about the other cars on the road. 'They're all such Sunday drivers,' she said fiercely, which made me laugh, she's such a bad driver. 'You look very thin,' I told her as I said good-bye, 'why do you eat so little?' She looked at me and blushed, very embarrassed and answered, 'They think I have cancer.'

'Oh Mother,' I began, but she shook her head as if to stop me from saying more. 'I'll be all right,' she said.

32

Jean and I agreed that it would be a great relief when all the holidays were over, that they were fine for numerous categories of people but that we didn't belong to any of them. New Year's Eve should be a big, wild party, or you should be alone with someone you love; neither of us, we said, wanted to go on a date with some young man to the Starlight Roof or some other Roof and have shrimp cocktails and American champagne and look at the clock every two minutes. She and I spent the evening together and were quite happy. I went over to her place in slacks, carrying my rollers in the pockets of my short coat, I took the bus and arrived half frozen, and we both washed our hair and set it. Then Jean cooked us dinner and we talked while watching television with half an eye. Around ten, a boy from a liquor store delivered a bottle of Dom Perignon, which Jean informed me is the most expensive champagne, from the client, with a card wishing us a happy New Year and saying that he was thinking of me and sorry we weren't together. I wasn't altogether happy with it, for it made me seem pathetic somehow, but we got high on it, which was good. At twelve, we turned off the television set, opened a window and listened to the whistles and the firecrackers. Then we kissed each other and heaved some deep sighs.

I went home around one, and had to walk awhile before I caught a taxi. The cabdriver had his radio going full blast, we wished each other a happy New Year, and then he said, 'And now back to school, no?'

'Yes,' I answered, 'worst luck.'

'My daughter is graduating this summer,' he said.

'Oh.'

'And you?'

'Next year, I hope,' I said.

That was a nice conversation to start the year with. In my saddle shoes and with my hair in a kerchief, I did look like a schoolgirl. When we got to my building, he didn't want a tip and wished me good luck once more. When he'd gone around the corner, I walked all the way along 86th Street to Lexington Avenue, bought the paper and a hot dog, and smiled on humanity, including even all those Germans there.

33

The client was not supposed to be back in town until after the New Year's weekend, but on Sunday at half past nine in the morning he called. He took me so much by surprise that I didn't recognize his voice; the conversation went:

'Happy New Year! Happy New Year, my sweet girl!' And me: 'Who is this?' Not very fortunate. But then he told me how he had of a sudden just not been able to wait another day to see me, and had taken a train into town on some excuse or other and could he please come over.

So I got up, started the coffee, took the rollers out of my hair and made the bed. Soon after, he showed up with a bag of croissants and the Sunday *Times*. He was wearing a dark sports shirt and a corduroy jacket, and he looked splendid.

Only when he walked into the room did I realize how glad I was to see him.

I asked, 'Did you miss me?'

'So much so, I thought I'd die – and I wanted to call you at midnight and then I thought I'd better not, that you might not appreciate that kind of sentimentality. Did you get my champagne?'

'Yes,' I said. I wasn't going to thank him for that keeping-a-mistress-quiet gesture. I amazed myself with that idea, it was surely strange to think of myself as the mistress of some married man.

'I'll heat the croissants,' I said, 'sit down and make yourself at home.'

'Did *you* miss *me*?' he asked.

I stuck my tongue out at him and vanished to the kitchen.

He sat in my chair, and I on the bed propped up with pillows, and we read the paper together. It was very snug.

'Don't fuss so,' I told him, 'don't be such a worry-bird.' That was because the client reading the newspaper always groaned and moaned and muttered things like: The stupid bastards, God how they twist things, why don't they – , and stuff like that. 'You don't know what they're up to now,' he said. 'They'll blow up the place yet, they just won't be able to resist it.'

And then I thought that I actually liked his protests. I had the sudden feeling that it was damn good to expect things to make sense and to get excited when they didn't. I kicked that idea around a bit; I felt I had got hold of something unusual for me. God, I said to myself, there are really people who can keep that up, and for a whole thirty years, or however long he's been reading.

'Why do you look so brooding?' he asked me. 'Do you know,' I said, 'that I sent five dollars last week to some women's peace movement?' I hadn't actually sent in yet, but I had kept their letter on my desk. Now I had to do it.

He lowered his paper and stared at me. Then he went back to it and said without looking up, 'We'll get married one day.'

'We will?' I asked. 'Are you proposing?'

'Would you accept?'

'Try me.'

He shifted in his chair. 'I'm not free,' he finally muttered. 'I will be one of these days,' he said.

'Well, you just missed your chance,' I said.

34

A while later, Susan came into the room, after first knocking although the door had been ajar. She was wearing a little black hat which looked frightening and told us she was going to a lunch and a matinée; and she had a cup of coffee with us. She directed cultural conversation at the client, and he gave me a wink as he answered her. I felt sorry for her then, and before she went out I made her change hats and take off her ear-rings in which pieces of green stone balanced little metal mermaids, and lent her a good string of pearls I have.

When she had pulled the front door shut behind her, the client started to do very bad entrechats and cried in an imitation of Susan's voice, 'I'm so disappointed by the modern ballet, aren't you? But don't you believe in the Oriental concept, the rhythms for instance hidden in the Mahabharata, the –'

I interrupted him. 'Poor Sue,' I said. 'Don't be so clever.'

He shrugged and sat down.

'Don't knock Susan,' I said, 'she's a girl after your own heart, she's a member of fifteen organizations and each lunchtime she is out picketing something or someone, she hasn't eaten lunch in months.'

'You're wrong there,' he answered, 'that's not a girl after my own heart, being a sloppy do-gooder. Anyway, I was just acting silly because I was so pleased to be alone with you. Let's go back to bed.'

I took off my housecoat and jumped into bed in my nightgown, turned my back towards the room and closed my eyes. I heard his shoes drop on the floor; he crept in behind me and fitted himself against me, his left arm around me. 'My feet are cold,' I said, and he put his under mine. We lay quietly, touching all the way from our feet up, very close and with his face in my hair. It felt wonderful and safe. I stayed motionless, and held his hand between mine, but I could feel his sex pushing against me. I told him not to stir, but of course it did not last. So I sighed and turned over on my back, and he kicked the covers off and came into me, and while in me, propped himself up and pulled my nightgown over my head, and fell down on me again. He was very fast, and I wanted him to be, for it was an anticlimax to me and I didn't particularly enjoy it. I had loved him while he lay behind me, feeling his body against mine. 'Did you really come?' he asked afterwards, and I made a face at him. Then he fell asleep. After a while I got up and dressed, and when he woke up, I served tea and toast, and brought him his tea tray in bed. It was darkening outside, and as we stopped talking for a moment, I could hear laughter from the street. I walked to the window and looked out. A group of people, in a cone of lamp-light, were with much fussing and joking packing themselves into a sports car. I stood there until they drove off and watched the tail lights bob up and down over the uneven pavement.

'Let's go on a long trip,' I said without turning.

'We've just come back from one,' he answered. I turned around at him.

'Don't look so dissatisfied,' he told me, 'I didn't mean Miami. I meant making love. Making love to you is like a voyage, you're a lovely and undiscovered country.'

'Oh screw,' I said.

He tried to put his arm around me as I walked past the bed, but I pulled loose and said, 'The border is closed.'

35

She was in love with him in those days or as close to loving a person as she could ever be. Being with him was a self-sufficient situation.

She was as pleased cooking for him as being taken to a good restaurant; for the first time she could understand a woman who worked for a man, helped him through college or something like that. Before, to her such behaviour had seemed treason in the war between the sexes. He was the one man with whom she had lost awareness of that war. But this peace was in force for her only when they were alone and isolated; when his ties with the rest of the world entered into it, the mood of their relationship changed immediately. In the beginning, they had both successfully kept the world at a distance: he because he didn't want to alienate her with his marriage; and she because almost by instinct she ignored what would hurt her.

She loved his body and she loved to excite him, not to feel the power she held over a man but simply because it pleased her to look at his face and study his expression of intense involvement when he made love to her or when she caressed or kissed him. She was completely free in making love with him, anywhere; he once made love to her from behind while she was working in the kitchen, and she liked that because she got the better of life by doing something not everyone had done. She got very excited herself, but now in a 'feminine' more than a masculine way.

She continued to refuse listening to his political harangues; yet she was, without telling him, coming to a point where she might suddenly involve herself with great energy in all these issues. One evening he had taken her to a Mexican movie in which an unspeakably poor (and unappealing) family struggled through various dismal adventures, and she had told him afterwards that she had hated it and that she knew already how dreary life could be and did not want to be confronted with that fact unnecessarily.

'Comes the revolution,' she had said, 'and we'll all be hanged anyway. And good riddance too.'

But in a strange way she had been thinking back to that evening, and had started using the word *revolución*, as those movie Mexicans had said it, for a private code: certainly not to mean any political revolution, but for what she called 'bothering' and people who bothered. One day, she told herself, I may join the *revolución*.

And she now lived in a 'show me' attitude towards him. He himself would have the power to make her believe in her *revolución* and to get her away from the idea that everyone was at heart a bastard anyway, so why bother. She greatly astonished him once at a party by entering into an argument and saying that the American system was *not* based on the idea that men were good, that it was based on the acceptance of men being bad, that is to say, interested in themselves only, and that the virtue of the system was that it made the best of that situation with a minimum of fuss and rules. She blushed as she said that, and refused to elaborate on it or say another word. She looked awkward then, vulnerable, as he had never seen her before, and just for one moment she was a girl who would inspire pity in a man.

She would have to believe in him first, before she could come out of the shell she had built around herself.

36

From a letter by the client:

. . . I'm writing you in a lonely and empty hotel room in a cold town. I assure you, nothing is emptier than a hotel room with a man alone in it. My bed looks dreary. If *you* were lying in it, peeking at me over the cover (or bedclothes as you call them) while I am writing at this desk, it would be like heaven. I'm sitting here and conjuring up your sweet face and your very beautiful body. I am torturing myself with those beautiful legs of yours, how they flash in their stockings when you walk ahead of me up my staircase. I hope you are being good and at home. I won't call you because I know I'll start worrying if you're not in, and I have no time for that, I have to go over my papers. From my room I look out over the main square of Providence. It's freezing like mad and there isn't a soul on the street. Nothing moves except a blinking neon sign across the hotel which makes it all even more cold and desolate. It's like the end of the world here. With you around, it would be the centre of the world. I love the east, west, north, and the south of you. I don't think I've written a love letter since I was sixteen – until I met you. I like it. Those goddamn telephones. I'm supposed to be back in New York tomorrow. Wednesday latest. I'll call you before six. I'll understand if you're not free. But I'll hate it. Be good. –

(I was free. He sounded harassed, as if he'd had a big scene about not being home that evening, so I said I was very tired and thought I should go to bed early.)

A letter from George:

London, 18 January

My Darling,

Thank you very much for your telegram wishing me a Happy New Year. I'm mostly glad because now I have an address, thank God, your office I assume. Well, better than nothing. Where have you been? Why cannot I have your home address? Are you living with some man? You must tell me, I have a right to know. You have been very cruel, but I forgive you. I know I have been a difficult person, and am sorry. I should have done things for you, like bringing you flowers, and worked harder, and helped you with things. I hope you will give me another chance. I have a job now in a drafting bureau, and I still study at night. I am doing quite well, and guess what . . . I even bought a car, a little Morris, but it's a car. Why don't you come back? I'll find a better place to live, and everything will be first-rate. You have no idea how much I have changed. I even cook dinner for myself and friends, and go to parties, send flowers to the hostess, and am quite a man about town. But I love you, and there is no girl like you.

Don't let me wait again for months without answering, please. I really insist, I don't want to be made a fool of. You don't want me to telephone your mother, I am sure, or your boss. Well, don't be so aloof then. You were my girl when you got on that train, and you still are.

I think about you very much. Do come back. Let me know if you need any money for that.

With much love,

George

My answer – not mailed:

Dear George,

F— you and your f— flowers.

37

I don't know when the client and I lost the innocence of our affair. You cross a line one day, but realize it only afterwards.

The flat tyre in Miami wasn't that line, although it *was* the end of that utter politeness people start out with and which I like even more, I think, than the greatest love affair. (It isn't so bad if it's slowly exchanged for intimacy and belonging, but if you don't love someone, or he is married, or some such little problem, you lose one without gaining the other.) I think we crossed a line the first time he mentioned his wife, conjured up her presence in my room, and made it impossible from then on for either of us to pretend that if he couldn't see me at any particular time, it was because of work. It was my fault that he talked about her: I suddenly couldn't stand the elliptical way in which he described his Christmas and New Year's Eve, and I forced him to use those words, 'my wife'. But I did manage to stop myself asking how she looked and what kind of woman she was, and whether, unlike me, she did bother about disarmament and the recognition of China.

What a pity. Jean suggested that I wouldn't be that interested in him if he were completely free and eager to drag me to the altar. But that wasn't true. Since I'd had this damn man, I indulged in more introspection than in my first nineteen years put together, and I knew by then that my egotism was limited. I didn't at all take it for granted or even think it likely that I would have luck in my life; I had settled long ago for plain rolling through. If the client had been free and proposed, I'd have jumped at it, and would probably have become so embarrassed at the blissfulness of it all that I would have started to get myself upset about the mess the world is in. (He would never have understood that. He would have thought I was faking it to please him.)

A line was crossed, and I began to baulk at his obscure little restaurants and tables in far corners out of sight. In his apartment, when his telephone rang, I'd pick it up and hand him the receiver. If he wasn't free one evening, I might even say that I wasn't free the next one and stay home without answering the telephone. And if he questioned me, I'd say that if he had his freedom, I wanted mine. I wouldn't do all these things all the time, of course; we had good days and bad days. Actually, if he was cheerful and tried to please me, I'd quickly enough tag along and let him get away with his dodges; if he acted morose and wronged, and dared to be jealous, he, a married man, I would feel like killing him. But if he then, instead of arguing and arguing, just said something to make me laugh, and embraced me, I would think, Oh, what the hell, who cares anyway, and I would smile again and tell him he could make love to me, and take off my dress.

38

Susan played a record all the time which haunted me and which I always associate with that winter. They still play it on juke-boxes, and then I see our street with the piles of dirty snow along the sidewalks, the steps up to our green door, the garbage cans with the lids tied to them with pieces of string, and our dilapidated but warm railroad apartment. I don't know the precise words, but we sang:

'The day that the rains came down,

Mountain streams swelled with pride' (or 'ran with blood') and then just 'la la la-la la-la la – la la la la la la.'

Once Susan burst into tears at that point. Why? She was in love with a painter, she told me. And he had said he was in love with her too, but he was going to Japan on a fellowship, so they had to say good-bye. 'Well, good riddance to him then,' I said. Susan sighed and said, 'Let's go to California. Wouldn't it be fun to drive out there together?' 'When?' 'In spring.' 'All right,' I said, 'I'll have seven hundred dollars saved by the end of March.' I wasn't sure I meant it, but neither was she. It was a nice plan to hold on to a bit.

So we began by giving a going-away party. Susan invited every man, woman, and child she knew, and I asked Jean who had somehow never met Susan. Then Jean said, could she ask common friends of hers and mine. Then there was the client to worry about. Jean and I agreed I shouldn't ask him; he was much older than everyone else, he would think they were all foolish boys, he would be ill at ease and make the others ill at ease. But he was the only person I didn't feel bored and restless with, and also I wanted to show him off.

Anyway, it became a lovely party. The client showed up early and brought me a lot of liquor and a cheese, and could stay only an hour. The guests who met him were slightly scared of him and they called him 'sir'. It pleased me.

Then later we played records and did nothing but dance. Very late at night the client called. Every drop had been drunk and everyone had gone except Jean, and a boy called Jerry who was lying on the floor; he was very sweet and funny, and completely harmless. He insisted on taking the phone but I don't know what these two talked about. The music was too loud and I went to have a look at Susan who was sick in the bathroom.

39

After that, the client and I had our first real, drawn-out fight. It started when he berated me about the party and this Jerry. Why had Jerry stayed behind, why was he lying on the floor, when did he go home, had he kissed me, and on and on. First I thought I just wouldn't answer and let him finish, but then he said, 'I see you don't want to talk about it.'

'There's nothing to talk about,' I screamed at him, 'why do you have to spoil it? We had a wonderful evening, I was proud of you, Jerry is a little queer who kissed me on my cheek when he left and told me you were very handsome and he hoped you and I would be happy.' And I burst into tears.

The client looked aghast at what he had done, but just as he opened his mouth, his telephone rang. He picked it up, and I marched into his bathroom and washed my face. I left the door open, and was sure after a minute that it was his wife on the line. His voice sounded self-effacing, as if he were trying to talk without being heard. I waited in the door of the bathroom and listened. He looked at me with some kind of shrug, and half turned away. 'Yes,' he said, 'that's wonderful. Thank you for thinking of it.' And, 'I don't know,' and 'Well, maybe later.' And then he laughed at something. I walked over to the bed, picked up my coat and put it back on, waved at him with a sickly sweet smile, and left.

I stood for a moment on the staircase, but I heard him still talking. When I was out in the street, he called me from his window, but I marched on and got a cab on the corner.

As soon as I opened my own front door, I heard the telephone ring, and it kept ringing at least ten times. Then, after a few minutes, it started again. I thought, That I can't take; so I turned off the gas under the dinner I had started for myself, put my coat on once more, and took a cab to Jean. I was lucky, I caught her as she was leaving to go to the theatre, and she gave me her key. I went upstairs and sat in her apartment, and made myself some tea. It was infuriating, there were so many chores I had to do in my own place that evening.

I went home at midnight; it was an expensive evening in taxi fares. Susan told me he had called several times and had said he'd call again in fifteen minutes. I asked her to tell him not to bother her further. She didn't quite put it that way, but she did say she wanted to go to bed now, and he didn't ring again. I did all my washing and ironing then, because I was wide awake, and didn't get to bed until four; I was very late for work the next morning and ready to spit blood, I was so mad at him; but he didn't call. The following day he sent roses and a letter, and when he called, I forgave him. He still asked, 'Where did you go to from my place?' but I didn't even let myself be annoyed with that, and told him I had gone to Jean because all that telephoning was driving me crazy.

We had a nice week after that, with some gay and festive evenings. He took me to an opening; I had bought a dress and looked quite marvellous. We went to a restaurant afterwards with a couple, friends of his, the first I met, and I think they were taken with me. I came to his place that night and stayed – the first and only time.

40

It was different from our travelling and motels, this going to his apartment to stay, and sleeping and waking up with him in his own bed. We came in, he turned on the light, and we looked at each other and decided we were very elegant, and somewhat high. For once, I didn't mind any of his tricks in that place, neither his turning off the telephone nor the letters and a photograph he scooped from his desk into a drawer. I felt very much that we were together.

'Dick said, "What a stunning girl" when we were waiting at the checkroom for you,' he told me. (Dick was the man who had been with us that evening.) He looked at me and added, 'I guess you are. It seems a pity almost to have you take that dress off.'

'I bought it at lunchtime,' I said, which seemed to surprise him. 'You mean, especially for tonight?' he asked.

I hung my dress carefully over a hanger in his bathroom. Then I cleaned his basin with a towel. I found a bottle of shampoo and told him I was going to wash his hair which was dirty; he protested halfheartedly and let me. So we puttered around in our underclothes; I sat at his desk in my slip and filed my nails, and thought that I had never before undressed with a man, like this.

I mean, it had always been taking off clothes for someone to make love to me. And putting them on again in the bathroom, and being uncomfortable because I was still dripping. And men were always embarrassed about being half-dressed themselves: justifiedly, because they looked rather uninspiring that way. Now, we were undressed because we were home.

He got into bed before me. As I went to take off my make-up, I saw that he had written on the bathroom mirror, 'I do love you,' and also a line in Greek. I asked him what it was. 'Nipson anomemata me monon opsin,' he said, 'in Greek letters it reads backwards the same as forwards.'

'What does it mean?'

'Wash off your sins and not just your face.'

'I have no sins,' I said, 'only men do.'

He made love to me and came very quickly, but I enjoyed it. I lay with my head on his shoulder and we started caressing each other, and after a while he came into me again. 'Now I'm invulnerable,' he said, 'I could stay this way all night.' That wasn't true, but it was a long time.

I woke up before him. His icebox contained one egg, a loaf of stale bread, and cans of condensed milk and coffee. I made a breakfast of French toast with that.

I went to my office in the black theatre dress and very high heels.

41

'You mustn't be mad,' the client told me, 'but I'm taking a couple of weeks' vacation.'

I was going to ask, Why should I be mad about that, but then I didn't say anything.

'I do need it,' he said. 'I'm going to Sarasota. I have worked very hard, and I'm run-down, I need to be alone and away from it all, believe me. My family, I mean, my daughter and my wife are staying home, she is in school, you know, my daughter – I'll just sit quietly in the sun, all alone, and do some work after a while, and I'll think about you. I'll be gone about three weeks, not more.'

'When are you going?' I asked. I wanted to say that I had a week's vacation coming up, but decided against it.

'The day after tomorrow –'

'Let's have a farewell party tomorrow together.'

'Well, you know, I can't tomorrow, I have to prepare so many things,' he said.

But he called the following day and announced he just had to see me before leaving. He came to the railroad apartment; he had bought me a little portable gramophone as a present, and he seemed really sad. I don't know why I became sad too; I hate good-byes; I had tears in my eyes as I put him in his taxi. 'Please be good,' he said, 'I don't know how I'll stand it without you for all that time.'

'That's your problem,' I said, but I kissed him on his mouth, which I never do.

It was quite a vigil.

I hadn't been cheating myself when I felt I was dating other men only to keep from brooding and waiting for his phone calls; with him gone, I lost all desire to go out. I'd slowly walk home from the office after six and I'd be the most abandoned waif in the world. I'd study the animated faces of the passers-by in the light from the shop windows; every girl held someone's arm, women were helped into cars by happy-looking men; and the people who were alone seemed to step determinedly, on their ways to meeting lovers or husbands or wives. Third and First Avenues were solid rows of headlights, all of cars homeward bound, hurrying to get there. I could visualize them driving through the early winter evening, in the bare countryside or along those endless blocks of Queens, towards *their* door – the single place, where they'd be expected, and embraced, listened to, handed a drink – and it seemed a miracle that of all these millions each one had someone who worked for him or her, who liked to touch her, feed her, listen to her little sorrows.

At that time, Susan never came in until late, for she was squeezing out the final days with her painter, and there I'd sit at my window without putting on the light. I called my mother every now and again, but I felt that it made her nervous; she imagined that I had been told she was dying and that I was sorry for her.

I would sit for hours without really thinking anything much. A human plant.

42

A telegram for the client came to our office; Jean took it in to her boss.

'It's some money matter,' she told me.

'Can it wait?'

'I'm supposed to call his home and read it to his wife,' Jean said.

'Shall I do it?' I suggested. It seemed intriguing to talk to her. 'Do you want to?' Jean asked. But I decided against it.

Later that day, I asked Jean, 'How did she sound?'

'How did who sound,' Jean said.

'The client's wife.'

Jean frowned, and she actually reddened.

'What is the matter with you!' I cried.

She shrugged. 'She wasn't there.'

'Well, where is she?'

'I don't know,' Jean said.

To hell with it, I thought.

At the end of the day, as we went down in the elevator together, I asked Jean, 'Is she in Sarasota with him?'

'Yes,' Jean said.

'Well, you can't win them all,' I said.

So I stopped vigiling.

43

The first day the client reappeared on the scene, we met at the Gotham for drinks after work.

'You look splendid with a tan,' I told him.

'Are you all right?' he asked. 'Why do you act so fishy? I so much longed to see you.'

I was tempted to ask him, had he been lonely, and lead him on along those lines, but only for a moment. I emptied my glass and asked for another drink.

'But you have changed,' he muttered. The cheerfulness on his face evaporated a bit. 'What happened? Did you fall in love with someone else?'

I sniffed.

'After that drink, I should go,' I said.

'Oh, you're not serious!' he cried. 'Aren't we going to have dinner together?'

'You've been away for a long time,' I answered, 'your wife must be counting on you tonight.'

'I don't care,' he began. 'She doesn't – ,' and then he turned purple. 'Did they – ?' he said.

Neither of us spoke while the waiter took our glasses away and put down new ones.

After a while, he started talking rapidly. 'You must let me explain,' he said. He waited for me to interrupt him, but I didn't, so he plunged on, 'When I told you I was going alone, I was telling the truth. So help me. Then at the last moment she decided to come along, she said she needed a rest too, and she had got someone to take care of Ellen. That's my daughter. What could I do? I couldn't say no. I didn't want her there. She just came. She had her own room, I told her I needed to be alone a bit.'

I looked bored.

'She left a week before me,' he declared, 'or almost a week. I even thought of calling you and asking you to fly down for a few days.'

'Why didn't you? I could have done with some of that sun, I'm as pale as a ghost.'

'I'm sorry, I'm really sorry now I didn't. I felt ... I thought that ...'

I directed my sickly sweet smile at him. 'You could have told them I was your daughter,' I said, 'I hear your wife is your age.'

He started to laugh, though a bit tremulously.

'Forget it,' I said. 'It's dinner time.'

44

My mother came to New York for two days to have some tests; she stayed overnight in the hospital and we had dinner together in her room. She looked better.

I walked home from there. I went over to the parapet along the East River and stared for a long time at the little icy waves reflecting the moonlight. I thought, Why am I happy that my mother looks better? She has never done anything for me, I could have dropped dead a year ago and she wouldn't even have known. Still, she is the only person in this world I'm tied to in some way, my only fixed point. There is more to it though. I understand her better now than I used to.

Indeed, why would she have worried about me? If love equals pain and then some, isn't it more sensible to stay clear of it all? Why would parents bother with children, or the other way around? That's creeping socialism too. If it's free enterprise we want, well, let's have it all along the line, I say. Every man, woman, and child for himself!

I felt very pleased with that. I could see myself delivering it as a speech from a soapbox on Hyde Park Corner. Then I became aware of a spooky man staring at me from a bench, and I marched on.

Perhaps more than a war between the sexes, there's a war between the generations, I thought. For themselves, old people live their no-holds-barred lives, but they pretend otherwise. Their rules and their morality are for keeping us in check. If they didn't do that, we'd upset their world in one day, and we would be happy – or at least, free. But they fool us just long enough. Eventually we see through the fraud, but then it's too late, by then we too are too weary and disillusioned for something really dramatic. Then we join the conspiracy, keep up appearances and help perpetuate the game to keep the next generation in line.

I wondered whether I'd hit upon a brilliant idea: I tried it on Susan when I came home. 'I think there are nice people at all ages,' Susan answered.

'And bastards.'

'Yes, sure. But that generations business is not serious. That's something the women's magazines live on.' Then she added, 'Did you have a fight with the client tonight?'

I began to laugh. 'Susan,' I said, 'you do me an injustice. You think my splendid philosophy is just the outcome of a quarrel with my middle-aged lover?'

The word 'lover' made Susan blush. She will call them 'boy friends' until she's ninety years old. 'He's only thirty-five, isn't he?' she asked.

At my Quogue beach party last summer (I don't know why I keep thinking about that silly party), a boy said to me when I told him I was nineteen. 'That's old, man.'

So now I looked at Susan and said too, 'That's old, man.'

45

One morning, it was suddenly like spring. It had rained hard all night, I had been lying in bed listening to it, and as I came out of the house the sky had blown clear and was green-blue, the colour of a kind of sherbet they used to sell from carts when I was a child. The snow and the mud had been washed away, even our street looked clean. Before I was at my desk, half a dozen people had told me, 'Nice day.' And so it was. That evening I tried out the California plan on the client, telling him that Susan and I were going to drive out there presently. He didn't say anything.

'Why don't you comment?' I asked. 'You look as if you were counting to a hundred before answering.'

He probably was, too; wondering whether to look sad or what.

'I'll go crazy without you,' he finally said. 'But – but I realize it would be very selfish of me to try to keep you here. I'm giving you a bad deal here.'

I do not know why those words made me so furious. 'That's my worry,' I spit out at him in a low voice. I hated him that moment – a bad sensation.

It gave him a shock. 'Well, you'll be back in New York, won't you?' he asked after a pause.

'Oh, go to hell,' I said and got up and walked out of his apartment – foolishly, because we were going to a movie I wanted to see, and I hated the thought of going home, it was such a lovely evening. So I skipped one green light at the street corner and let him catch up with me. He put his arm through mine and we walked down Lexington Avenue without speaking.

Twilight was falling rapidly.

At 57th Street, a girl I'd once talked to for a few minutes at a party stood next to us waiting for the light. She recognized me and said hello very warmly, and peered at the client.

He shivered; he had run after me without a coat.

'Don't catch a cold,' I said.

'I'm so sorry darling,' he said softly. 'Please be patient with me. I'm in a bit of a trap. But I'll manage. All's well that begins well.'

'Oh, you,' I answered and shrugged, and smiled at him.

We sat in the movie house and held hands. He took his hand out of mine and stroked my leg. 'Don't go to California,' he said. 'Don't. I want you here.'

A lady sitting in front of us turned around and said, 'Ssh.'

'Promise me you won't go,' he whispered.

I took his hand back in mine. 'We'll talk about it later,' I said.

46

The following Sunday Susan and I bought a car. We didn't mean to, not so fast, but we looked at the ads, called someone, were persuaded to come out to Long Island, were met at the station by him in a white Ford convertible, and bought it. The car was four or five years old, but it looked nice and solid; the man wanted four hundred and fifty dollars and that's what we paid, but we got him to go to his garage with us and have them put on new tyres. It was a big car; in England people would have stopped and stared at it. He told us to keep his plates until we had new ones, and we drove straight off. When we were out of his sight, I made Susan stop. 'I'm going to put the top down,' I said. 'But it's freezing.' 'Never mind,' I said, 'the fresh air will do us good. You can wear my scarf.' So we drove into town in an open car. At the stoplights we were whistled at. Susan enjoyed it too, although she kept looking straight ahead. A truck driver lowered his window, elaborately leaned out and shouted, 'Need someone to warm your hands, girls?' I stuck my tongue out at him, and Susan crunched the gears as she took off. 'Watch it,' I said, 'this creature has to get us to California.' 'It feels very good,' Susan said, 'I don't think we were gypped.' I didn't want to drive it yet, I had to get a New York licence first.

We had a lovely afternoon washing the car. Susan's painter came to look at it and he, too, thought that it was a good buy. Then we went to find a parking space for it, locked it up, and walked home. I wanted to leave Susan alone with her painter, so I went over to Jean's, but that evening I came out to have another look at our car before going to bed. I was dying to take off to California in it; I would have liked to leave the next morning. I was afloat again.

47

The last weeks with the client were sweet and almost nostalgic. We were on our best behaviour and there were no more arguments, no more stalking out of places by me: like our beginning, but only outwardly. Then our getting-on was innocent, now it was intentional. It all amazed me; this affair had lasted such a short time really, and yet it had gone through all these stages, and seemed the only thing, sort of, that had happened in my life so far. I don't think he knew what to make of it. He seemed half-relieved that I'd be off his hands, and at the same time stricken by the idea of losing me. Heaven knows, probably people can feel both things at the same time. He made me a list of names, friends he had in Los Angeles and San Francisco, which I kept with my papers; but I never thought beyond the trip itself. I just wanted to be on the road, 'away from it all', as Susan said. She had found a girl who would take the apartment until the building was to be torn down, later in the year, and I sold her the bits of furniture I had collected. Most of my winter clothes and whatever books and objects I wanted to hold on to, I put in a locker which I shipped to my mother for storage. I didn't consult her about it beforehand and later found that it had been a stupid move. So there I was, ready for anything, with half a car, four hundred dollars, a suitcase, a hat-box, and freedom interspersed with moments of panic.

I had to quit my job almost a week before we were leaving, and those free days of mine the client and I drove all over the countryside. I actually counted, this is our last Tuesday together, our last Wednesday, and so on – I don't know whether he was as aware of things. He started many sentences he never finished; I imagine he would have liked to say we weren't going to part, but couldn't quite make it. At least he was honest then. He sounded different about the world, too; he didn't talk about its sorrows any more. Justice, injustice, all those burning issues – 'To hell with it all,' he said once, 'I wish I had a lot of money, or I wish I were a playboy. I just want to lie on a beach in the south of France with you. You'd look great in a bikini.'

'I bought one for California,' I told him. He didn't like that idea. 'Will you be faithful to me while you're there?' he asked. A very silly question. 'Once Susan and I are on the road,' I said, 'I don't want to look at another man for the rest of my life,' which was a nicer answer than he deserved.

48

Our next to last afternoon; he and I had lunch in an empty restaurant, pseudo-French and dreary. We sat staring into space until after three o'clock, with the client smoking one cigarette after another, and the waiter in a stained white jacket fidgeting around us, emptying the ash tray, pouring the last drops of coffee out of the *café filtre* pot and letting its lid drop on our table.

Finally we got ourselves up and out of there, and stood in the street. We were somewhere north of Columbus Circle, a grey and dirty block of garages and oil-streaked asphalt; old newspapers blew through the gutters; it was a dismal scene. The sky was leaden and it was already getting dark. He sighed. I turned towards him: he looked pale and old, with rings under his eyes. Unexpectedly, I felt sorry for him, I almost pitied him; I didn't know why and I had never had that feeling towards him before. I wanted to say, Don't be sad, it's all right, life isn't that important; and take him in my arms and rock and soothe him.

'Well, I guess I should put you in a cab,' he said halfheartedly.

I answered, 'No, you come with me, we're going to get my car.'

I made him sit on the right, turned on the heater and the radio which both worked, and drove him over the George Washington Bridge and up on the parkway along that side of the Hudson. It is the most silent area near New York I know; the rearview mirror was empty. I drove well.

I stopped at a roadhouse and made him go in and get himself a drink. I waited in the car. I don't know why the hell *I* have to pamper *him*, I thought. But that's how it was.

When he came back, he looked more appealing; I patted him on his arm and on we went. The next time I stopped was at some kind of look-out point, off the road. There wasn't a soul there, and as I turned off the lights, we could see the dark gleam of the river. I tried to undo his belt but almost broke a nail. 'Take off your trousers,' I said. 'What?' he asked, but then he complied. 'Women have more grace taking off clothes than men,' I told him. I bent over him and began kissing him, very carefully. At one point he started to say something, but I said, 'Lean back and be still.' I used my hands too, I was endlessly patient, like a prize harem girl of an ancient sultan. When I saw he was almost there, I stopped and waited, and he groaned. Finally I took his sex in my mouth and cupped my hands around the rest of it. I felt the swelling of its point, and then he came; I almost choked but it was exciting. After a moment, he pushed me away and struggled back into his clothes. 'That was lovely, where did you learn that,' he murmured, with his eyes closed. I grinned. I think I felt better than he did. He pulled out a handkerchief and started fussing with it.

'Oh stop that,' I said, 'Nipso no nipso nenono nipso.'

He laughed then, finally. 'Nipson onomema me monon opsin,' he said. And then he put his arms around me, pressed me against him, and suddenly began to cry.

'Oh dear,' I said, 'poor ducky dear. Cheer up, ducks.'

And so we went back to New York. He drove, and I lay with my head in his lap, half dozing. When we got to the Bronx or whatever it is, the car entered a grid of light from the street lamps; I looked up at his chin which was all I could see of his face, except when he looked down at me, with a wistful kind of smile.

49

Not until after Washington do you have the sensation of being on the road – *la grand' route* of that French song. The first stretch out of New York or most of it I had done before, and it's like city driving anyway, hemmed in somehow. But then, in Virginia and going west, no more client, no more New York, that whole little life gone. It had been very sweet, and gone sour, and good riddance to it.

'Would you hand me the map?' Susan asked. That girl was driving in a very un-beatnik manner, more like a Trailways chauffeur on a schedule; she had even wanted to make reservations ahead in motels until everyone assured her that wasn't necessary in March. She was comforting; she worried about the easy things. The back seat was strewn with stuff of hers: at the next stop, she had promised, she was going to sort it out and pack it properly. The weather was cold and wet; gusts of rain hit the windshield and stuck wet leaves to it. But the car purred beautifully.

I sat there with my head empty; occasionally a thought would drift through, like 'Perhaps I'll phone my mother tomorrow' or 'I still owe the cleaners two dollars.' Apart from that, I didn't think beyond the nice solid doors and roof and dashboard of our car: I traced the curlicue on the glove compartment and stared intently at all the licence plates on the back of a truck we trailed.

It was Sunday; the little towns we went through looked deserted. 'Imagine living here,' Susan said as we rolled through an empty main street with puddles, a five-and-ten, a lunch counter, a movie house, and a new hardware store decorated with little flags flapping in the wind. Imagine that being the centre of your universe, your point of reference; it was all so ugly. Under the marquee of the movie house, which looked closed, a girl was standing alone. Her eyes caught mine for a moment. Was she waiting for a boy friend who hadn't shown up? Was she just standing there to be away from her parents' overheated living room where they were watching television and drinking beer? I looked back; she turned up the collar of her beige raincoat and followed our car with her eyes. 'I'm sure if we stop and offer her a lift to California, she'll hop right in as she is,' I said. Susan, busy with a railway crossing and a sheriff watching her quietly from a police car parked on the corner, didn't hear what I said and just smiled. Then the houses ended, the RESUME SPEED sign appeared, and fields of black earth on each side of the road. 'Back in civilization,' Susan announced. Every now and again she came out with a remark like that which made me like her very much.

50

They were having tea with lemon in a drugstore in Lebanon, Illinois, just east of St Louis, when Susan showed her where they were on a map of the entire United States. And suddenly she was overwhelmed by the feeling of distance. 'My God,' she muttered, 'we're only at a third. Look at that chunk of land, look at those huge states.' All at once she felt exhausted. It seemed too much, beyond her capacity, to venture forth in that territory which was so empty of names on the map. She was frightened. If it hadn't been for Susan, she would have turned around right there. 'Are you all right?' Susan asked. 'I'm a bit sick to my stomach,' she answered, and Susan made her swallow an Alka-Seltzer. I'll be OK once we're in California, she thought, when you're near the sea you're never lost. That's why New York didn't seem strange, it was right on the same Atlantic. Now I just have to hold my breath while we plunge across all this land.

When they were back in the car, she talked about this fear to Susan, who was not impressed. 'There's nothing to worry about,' Susan said. 'We're sticking to a federal highway, there's always a gas station near, a phone booth, a doctor, a hospital, the whole bit.' 'But that's not what I mean at all,' she protested, but she felt unable to explain what exactly frightened her.

It stayed with her as they drove through the prairie states, this sensation of being swallowed up by an unfathomable quantity, like drowning; she felt that if she would get out of the car and walk away, no one would ever hear of her or see her again. The car was the lifebuoy. And this sensation stopped being only fear; it became strangely tempting to do just that, it appeared like a soothing, painless suicide. She played endlessly with the idea during the long hours of driving: how at a gas stop in some little town, she would wait for Susan to go to the ladies room, and then she'd sneak off, hide somewhere in a store or a cinema. She could see it, Susan puzzled and worried, driving up and down the street, questioning people. Finally Susan would give up and go on. Then she'd take a room in that clapboard little hotel across from the depot they had just passed, under another name of course. Who on earth would ever find her there? Or she'd rent an apartment somewhere on a second floor, over a store in the shopping street or over a bar. In these fantasies she was a whore. She didn't know why, but she could *obviously* not conceive of herself as being, say, a typist for that place there, the Eureka Feed Company; but she could be the local call girl of Eureka, Kansas. She would never tell anyone her name; in fact she wouldn't speak. Men (she visualized them looking like the actors in a western) would come to her table in the bar, size her up, and pull out their money. They all knew she wanted to be paid in advance. Then they'd walk over to her place; 'What's your name, honey?' they'd ask, but she wouldn't answer, just smile vaguely. They'd make love to her (she didn't dwell on that at all in her thoughts), and she'd go back to the bar, where her drink was still untouched on her table, beside the paperback she was reading. After a while she'd move on. She'd buy a canvas bag at the five-and-ten, which would hold all she needed, put on jeans, and get on a bus. She thought of the lonely girl under the theatre marquee in the rain, in the town in Virginia, and now she felt a pang of jealousy for her. Perhaps they'd meet and travel together. Maybe to Mexico. That was the final, total vanishing. However, there was no proper ending to be thought of. Saving, or getting, lots of money and reappearing in the world wasn't a good ending at all. It was a dream of going down: of ending up in a nameless slum somewhere in a tropical city. But that was where the image blacked out, too: she couldn't visualize herself older than she was now, fat or flabby, or with dirty children around her.

She was a gloomy companion while this went on in her mind; she surprised Susan by saying very little and being oblivious to the driving, to what they ate or where they slept. She apologized for it and said it was because she didn't feel well.

Then one morning she announced, 'I'm cured.' They were in

New Mexico, the weather had turned sunny and dry; the landscape and the buildings – different from anything she'd ever seen – looked familiar to her. It's a young country, she thought, we're back in my time.

'I think I'll like California,' she said.

'Well,' Susan answered, 'glad to have you with us again. You'd gotten me worried. Here, you drive, I'm going to have a nap in the back. I'm sleepy.'

So with Susan hidden in the back seat, she drove on, going fast, singing to herself, 'Albuquerque, Albuquerque, Albuquerque,' and feeling very happy.

51

I took a fancy to California. That drive from New York across the whole country wasn't as exciting as I had thought; in fact, everything but the tail end was pretty miserable for me. I don't know why I didn't feel like a Quogue kid in the car with all that space in front of me; since Quogue, that kind of freedom had seemed to me what it was really all about, the Great Adventure, the best America had to offer. Perhaps I was, at twenty, too old; or too much of a coward. Anyway, I was sorry once we got to California that I hadn't been with it more and I promised myself to do better next time. As soon as we were in California, as soon as the man at the state line had checked on whether we weren't bringing in boll weevils or orange bugs, Susan started to gripe and I to defend anything and everything. What horrified her, amused me – everybody, no matter what their jobs, being *really* actors; the supermarkets open through the night; the idiocy of the traffic; all those things. I could see Los Angeles was ugly, but I thought it was an honest and twentieth-century kind of ugliness, without pseudo-European icing. When we reached downtown, just arriving, around noon, newsboys were selling extra editions: we got worried because of the fat headlines, and it turned out to be some local actor's family scandal. And not only that; the rest of the world was buried at the bottom of page eleven. It's a superficial town, I guess, but the superficiality goes right to the core, and can therefore, as I pointed out brilliantly to Susan, no longer be called superficiality.

Susan and I had had our only wrangle of the whole trip when we went to the Montecito Hotel, a name the client had given me, and probably the best turn he ever did me. I asked for a cheap room. As it turned out we got a whole little apartment for so much less than New York that I felt entitled to settle down at the pool and wait a few days before going job hunting. But when we got upstairs, Susan told me sternly that I should have said 'inexpensive' instead of 'cheap'. I laughed at her, and for some reason she got very mad.

I didn't give in, I hate this living in genteel euphemisms.

Anyway, we put ourselves in the sun and relented all around. Susan had been in San Francisco but never in Los Angeles; she agreed it was a place without big-city blues. After three days we both looked marvellous; she even let me drag her to a hairdresser one morning and came out a new woman. Everyone in the hotel came to talk to us; they were show-business people, some phoney, most of them nice. She and I could have had a fine time together. Then unfortunately – for me – Susan got a telegram from her painter in Tokyo, forwarded by her parents. He was asking her to come over and marry him. It shook her up completely; she came back to her chair at the pool in tears and as she handed me the telegram without a word, I expected to read of some disaster. She asked me what to do and I answered, of course, that I had no idea.

'With all those geishas around,' I said, 'it seems to me pretty much like carrying coals to Newcastle, as we called it in school.'

That stopped Susan's tears and she gave me an indignant look.

'I mean,' I added hurriedly, 'that it probably proves it isn't just sex, but he really loves you.'

Well, two days later she was off, which is what would have happened no matter what I'd said. I kept the car and was to pay her back her share as soon as I had a job. I drove her to the airport and we had a touching farewell. I must admit I felt terrible driving back into town alone; it all seemed so vast and merciless suddenly, quite different. But the following morning I set out bright and early to find a job. I landed one before the week was out, and was back once more behind a typewriter, though the ribbon of this one, very un-New Yorkish, was green.

52

My next boy friend was someone called Al. He was twenty-three and a disc jockey for KESM, a tiny radio station at the edge of town, but they listened to it in Los Angeles. It paid Al five hundred dollars for playing records from seven to midnight, six evenings a week. I met him on one of his seventh evenings at a messy party in the Montecito: a neighbour of mine celebrating that he had gotten a part in a television serial. The meeting wasn't love across a crowded room. I was pestered by a drunken, ageing actor; I can handle a thing like that, but he was a bit too much for me. And so when this Al came into the room just then, with a shy and somewhat lost air, I marched over, attached myself to him and showed him to the bar. He was a pale, dark, young man, looking almost like a gypsy, with a childish face but not unattractive. I was, in low heels, still taller than he. We talked only about popular music, but he was cheerful company. He was a splendid dancer, much better than I, and he led me along fine. I left early; I had a long working day and a long drive to and from the office behind me. I promised Al to come to the studio one evening and listen in, and that's how it began.

It was interesting to watch him at work, it's soothing to see a man *in command* of things, no matter what they are. Afterwards there was a whole crowd, mainly musicians, and we all went to a café on the Strip and drank beer. I was exhausted when I finally got back to the Montecito but it had been a fun evening. I hadn't for a long time been with people who didn't take things too seriously. Then there came a free weekend for Al, and he asked me along to Palm Springs. We went in three cars, including mine; we were ten people. And when we got there, we just naturally distributed ourselves over the hotel rooms; everyone seemed so completely to take it for granted that Al and I would share a room, that I ended up feeling the same. They made you feel that it didn't matter, that it was idiotic to make a fuss about a thing like that, and in that particular mood and the way they looked at things, indeed it did not matter. We had a long evening in a night club, and when he and I found ourselves back in this room, we just undressed and got into bed; after a minute he stubbed out his cigarette, kissed me on my mouth and crept on top of me. I helped him; and he made love to me, and we fell asleep; and that was that. The following morning he was up and out of the room before I woke up; and when I came down to breakfast wearing shorts, everyone said I looked great, and I got an equally warm welcome from the whole group. We went swimming after that and Al sat with me, but there were no private looks between us or any other kind of hanky-panky. So it went, it was a peaceful time. They were a simple bunch of people, kidding each other in the most ingenuous way, without malice, with lots of laughing. Sunday evening they drove me home first, since I had to get up early, and Al parked my car for me at the Montecito and then they all kissed me good night and off they were.

In my cubicle at the reception desk was a picture postcard from the client, saying, Hope you had a nice trip, thinking of you, love.

53

My television neighbour took me to dinner at the house of an old lady who had once been a terribly famous movie writer. Her name was Gyor, she was a Hungarian. There's a big supply of jokes about the craziness of show-business Hungarians, or so I gathered at that dinner, but she was a calm, dignified woman who told me that I was 'a pretty child'. It made me feel like curtsying to her. This lady, living in a ramshackle house, had dozens of cats, and when she saw I liked them, she offered me a kitten. I'd never had one before; I slightly mistrust people with pets, they usually go on so about them. But this was different; it was a very sweet creature, all grey, and tiny, and it didn't have a name yet. I decided I wanted it, and would call it Gyor after its owner. She approved, and lent me a basket to smuggle it into the Montecito. So I acquired my new room-mate, a movie cat.

I had moved to a smaller apartment in the hotel after Susan had flown off for her Far East romance, and I was quite neatly installed. I loved my white car which I washed once a week, and my cat. I had the gramophone the client had given me at my bedside, and every time I went grocery shopping I bought a record. I didn't get home from work before seven, but everything was open late, and except for parties there aren't many places to go to in Los Angeles anyway. All you need there are some cotton dresses and straw shoes. I hate getting up early but coming out into the street the world never hit you the way it does in New York; the sky was blue and the air balmy, you drove off with the top down, left your laundry on the way, ambling along, with palm trees lining the streets, and everyone tanned and smooth looking. Of course, a typewriter with a green ribbon is still a typewriter.

Saturdays I would see Al and his friends; I'd wait through his show and then we'd go out. I would stay with him, he had a ranch-style house all on his own, quite big, in the Hollywood Hills. You drove ten minutes from the boulevard, and suddenly you were in wild country, steep slopes overgrown with shrub, and scattered houses on stilts, each tied to the world by an electric cable. It was wonderful going up there at night, through the inky dark, with the houses little ponds of light and music.

It was my 'Desafinado' time; a record I had bought in the supermarket for one forty-nine and played as soon as I came home, every day. Its title means 'out of tune', I don't know why. It haunted me. I danced through my room to it, clutching the little cat, looking like an idiot, but not minding.

54

Al asked me to help him cook a Sunday brunch and I said yes, ill-advisedly, for I have never had to look at so many eggs in my life. He must have had fifty people in.

Here's how their conversations went:

One man: 'Half the trouble is, people don't understand what the other person's talking about. All diplomats should speak English.'

Second man: 'Why English? Because we speak English? Don't be such an egotist, Mark. French would be better.'

Mark: 'Why?'

Third man: 'Because that's what most people in the world speak.'

Second man: 'Exactly.'

Mark: 'Oh.'

Second man: 'There's that fellow who had a plan for a world language, an artificial language, so nobody would be at a disadvantage. That was clever.'

Third man: 'Zolotow you mean. That was just a lot of mishugas.'

Fourth man: 'Sam Zolotow? I know that guy.' (They ignore him.)

This was very tiring, for I knew they were wrong, about French I mean, but I didn't know what was the right answer and so I couldn't say anything. Suddenly, I thought of the client. He would surely know which language is spoken most in the world. It was strange, that was the first time I spontaneously thought about him, and missed him. I wanted him there, just to tell them. Then it passed.

But as they got back to talking about music, they were all right. They played clubs, which are try-out recordings they had made, and which they carried around with them. They asked me which ones I liked and disliked, and although I don't know a thing about music, I told them. I made them laugh, but they listened to me.

A girl played the piano, and Al told me to sing a British song, but I said the only song I really knew was –

> We are Siamese if you please.
> We are Siamese if you don't please.

I told him I was the only girl in Los Angeles who did not want to be in show business.

55

This Al showed himself to be totally different from what you might expect at first. He kept late hours of course, but once you got used to that, it was about as odd, or way out, or whatever the term is, as knowing a night watchman. He rarely drank anything but beer and counted the number of cigarettes he smoked a day. As for smoking pot, as music people are supposed to do, he'd sooner fly to the moon; and when I started dating him, there didn't seem to be any ex-girl friends around; he was really what his friends called a good guy. They also said he was a swinger but with them that just meant he didn't play rock 'n' roll but had a notion of good music. I liked it, except for the way he went to see his mother all the time. I could have done without that, for I think he waited for her to tell him when to have his hair cut and when to blow his nose. So here was this glamorous radio man who seemed to be slightly scared of me, a rotten secretary, and who thought that I was a very jazzy character.

I had known him four weeks when he said one night, 'Honey, why don't you move in with me? We'd be much better off. And I'm not home too often.' We were sitting in his car, parked on Franklin Avenue in front of the Montecito, and it was two in the morning. I had just, involuntarily, frustrated an attempt of his to kiss me good night, by yawning without stopping. I'd been up since seven-thirty that morning.

I thought that over. I calculated, coolly, that it would save me thirty dollars a week rent, and most meals probably. I'd have a much longer drive to the office, and the expense of the gas for that. But I'd end up as an unpaid housekeeper, more likely than not, cooking meals at one in the morning and washing dishes. Not such a good idea.

I decided not to answer, I just smiled and got out of the car, I walked around it and kissed him through the window.

He took hold of my wrist. 'No, honest,' he asked, 'why not?'

'Well, for one thing,' I said, 'you'd keep me up till one or two, and I'd have to get up again at some ungodly hour like seven to get to my office in time. I'd be a wreck after a week.'

'Office?' he said. 'But that's not what I meant. You don't have to go to any office. You can fiddle around, I'll take care of things. You'd be my girl, officially sort of.'

I blushed then. 'I'll think about it,' I muttered, and I ran in. He'd never have guessed, but I blushed because I had misjudged him and because I had been such a little bitch in my calculations. I was shook up; I said to myself that he was the first person in my life, the absolutely first one, who had volunteered to take care of me. I almost loved him for that. If it hadn't been for Gyor my cat, I'd have started crying once I got to my room.

That cat always cheered me up immediately.

56

She had bypassed her hotel going home, and was driving along Sunset Boulevard; below her, on her left, the city made a network of lights against the tight blue sky. She had a band in her hair, but the wind tugged at its ends and she slowed down. She came to a stop at a traffic light and stared mesmerized at a yucca tree reflecting the colours of a neon sign. Then somcone behind her started honking his horn.

It was a beautiful evening.

She had done her work badly that afternoon, sitting behind her desk in a daze, and when she dropped her eraser it took her ten minutes before she could decide to pick it up.

Now she was driving her car in a not quite conscious effort to recapture the mood in which she had come to Los Angeles, the last stretch from Albuquerque to Phoenix and from Phoenix to here. She told herself that she was a lucky girl. She was going down Sunset in a white convertible (which already two thirds belonged to her). She had a tan, she was twenty, and she was in *glamorous California,* as Jean would have said in a thick accent with heavy L's. She smiled, thinking of Jean. She was fancy-free and free. The Quogue kids would have been impressed seeing her go by. Not to mention her friends in London. If they could see her now . . .

It didn't work.

She was in a fog and couldn't clear her vision. It all seemed so far away, New York, London, her mother, the client, everything. Nothing was quite real. Al was a sweet boy, but he wasn't real; an evening with him was like going to a double feature, she thought, passing the time, painlessly. Well, dammit, she said to herself. My cat's real. Screw it all. A bit of self-irony is needed. Who cares? Is it so important to be happy, or loving, or loved?

To hell with me. I should be of service somewhere, be a nurse, or a teacher, or work for the *revolución*. She shrugged. If it's unimportant whether I'm happy, she thought, then it's equally unimportant whether a million me's, a million Korean orphans or Bolivian tin miners are happy.

What I've got is called spleen in old novels. *Le cafard.* It's a rich girl's disease. A disease of fat and silly people.

She pulled up behind a line of cars waiting at a car-wash place. She liked standing behind the glass partition watching the machine splashing and drying her car. After this, I have to buy some cat food, she thought, and then I'm going home and read in bed.

'Close your top, miss,' a garageman shouted at her. She gave him a smile. 'Why don't you help me with it,' she said sweetly.

57

I did it. I packed gramophone, cat and caboodle, and moved in with Al.

I didn't give up my job yet. That seemed a bit much; I couldn't quite visualize myself asking him for household money. Thus we didn't see very much more of each other. I had my own bedroom, because I didn't want him to wake me when he came home. He often did, anyway, creeping into bed with me. I'd wake up because he'd caress me, but I wouldn't wake up completely; it was nice to be made love to that way, have a man hold you and come into you while you're in this warm trance, and then feel him come, and after a while he tiptoes away. Before going to bed himself, Al put out a breakfast tray for me with cereal and coffee ready to heat, and my cat had a splendid time running around in the garden. When I came home in the evening she would duck out from some bush and make a dash for me – like a dog – and then run by, and we'd chase each other. I know I'd hate it if I saw someone else carry on like that, but this was different. Gyor was no ordinary cat.

I didn't feel the need to tell them in the office I was living with someone, so I kept the Montecito as my official address. They were nice people there, and told me I could still come and use the pool. At times I drove by during lunch if the boss was out, or after work. My very first morning in Al's house, a Saturday, the Montecito receptionist telephoned me and told me someone had called for me from New York, first at eleven in the evening, and then three or four more times during the night. There was no message, but the night clerk had said it was a man.

That would of course have been the client. The swine would pick the first night I wasn't in, for that.

The receptionist was a good professional hotel man, he didn't laugh or show any reaction. I didn't know what to tell him, though. 'If they call again, shall we say you're out of town, miss?' he finally suggested, and I said that was a perfect idea. Thank heaven Al was out when this call came; he had gone to get his car lubricated. Or perhaps he had just wanted me to have a chance to wander around in his place alone and get settled; he was a thoughtful boy.

58

Things coincided. I was late for work twice in a row and got a wicked upbraiding which turned into a big scene, with my boss, purple in the face, looking as if he were going to strike me. I had talked back because I hate being shouted at; then I became actually frightened and walked out. I came back after lunch and he had put another girl behind my desk. My colleagues told me I shouldn't have walked out for now I didn't qualify for unemployment. They weren't too sympathetic about the whole thing. I hadn't liked that job anyway. But right then Al started an offensive for me to quit working, and I gave in. I hesitated a long time, and did it only because this, too, was so much a normal situation in his crowd that you felt silly fighting it.

The reason I hesitated was not that I liked working; I do not. I am lazy and moreover hate sitting behind a typewriter or taking dictation in a cloud of cigar smoke all day long while my time on earth rolls by. And I didn't hesitate either because I was afraid of being under obligation to Al. I wasn't. I felt he was getting himself a good deal. I hesitated because I knew it was somewhat lower-class. 'What do you do?' 'Nothing, I'm Al's girl friend.'

Oh well.

He was serious about this, he really enjoyed the responsibility. He sent me to the hairdresser, and gave me a charge account at Jax and that kind of thing; he was always forcing money on me. But I was a good hostess and his friends were very impressed; you could see that they wondered how he had done so well for himself.

Now I'd go to his studio about every other night, and we'd all go out after, or I'd stay home with my cat and read.

The way he talked made me laugh. He and his closest friends

weren't corny, though they had a kind of humour which provided a pat phrase for every situation. Everything was made relative that way; it took the sting out of things. It's hard to think of an example; say someone's house burned down, they wouldn't lament with him, but tell him, 'Christ, the things you do to get into the paper.' At a party where a girl was being slightly pawed by someone, her boy friend came over and asked the man, 'Are you checking her oil?' Not very funny, but there was something habit-forming about this attitude.

They never talked about politics and indeed rarely about anything or anyone outside Los Angeles. And the world's turmoils and despairs, which the client had worried about so, were, to them, simply cooked up by the commies to annoy the United States. I missed my fat Sunday *Times*, but I still read whatever paper Al got Sunday morning; after ten minutes he'd want to go out, or do something, for he only read the sports page. I berated him the same way the client used to berate me; but he only smiled or said, 'I'm just a hick, baby.'

59

The last hours of the day were the best.

When Al had gone to his job, she would bring her chair to the terrace and sit there looking out over the canyon. The evening air carried sounds from invisible sources: car doors slamming, dogs barking. In between it was very still. Opposite her, across the canyon, stood a half-finished ranch house. No one was working on it, but a group of boys sometimes played there. They looked like juvenile delinquents and their presence annoyed her, until one evening when one of them, who had been screaming at the others, suddenly started to cough, pitifully, and finally walked away when he couldn't stop. The others left too, then. They were just children.

The sun set behind that house, in a rim of pine trees on the hill which turned red in the last light. It was very beautiful.

It seeemed to her there as if the sky, once darkness fell, slowly descended, peacefully covering the earth and her with it like a blanket. She felt content and, beyond that, an urge to give love, to embrace the whole world.

60

The next time I went to the Montecito to sit at the pool and work a bit on my tan, they had a whole batch of letters there from the client. There was something threatening about all that mail, envelopes marked with a red *please hold* or *please forward.* The man on duty at the desk promised me he'd return future mail with a notice, LEFT WITHOUT FORWARDING ADDRESS.

Then I still found myself in my deck chair with all those letters I didn't have the nerve to open. One was a picture postcard and I read it after a while. He had pasted some lines on it, cut from a book or a magazine: 'When I think of your lovely body, I don't give a damn about Central Europe'. 'These words', the client wrote, 'are from a letter written to his mistress by a French diplomat at a conference in Geneva. I feel precisely that way; I don't give a damn about Central, West, or East Europe, Africa, Asia, or America. I like that Frenchman. I'd like to think that those conferences never get anywhere for such good reasons. They're good reasons. Your body is the most important thing in the world.'

It was a disturbing postcard. I hoped the hotel man hadn't read it, that would be maddening. I didn't read any more, I took the whole batch to the garage which was beside the pool and put it in the ash can. Doing that, I felt like a criminal getting rid of a pistol or something. Then I went back to my chair. It was very warm in the sun.

I fell asleep. I had promised to telephone Al at noon to wake him, and when I opened my eyes it was past two o'clock. I went to call him and he wasn't angry; he said, 'I guess you forgot,' and I apologized and told him I'd fallen asleep.

When I had hung up, I stood in that telephone booth for a minute, staring at the patterns made by the water on the flagstones around the pool. It was very still, you could hear the sound of a truck climbing up the avenue.

I picked up the receiver and put in a collect call to the client. I heard his surprised voice as he interrupted the operator to say, 'Yes, yes, I accept the call.' 'Where have you been?' he immediately began. 'Where are you? Didn't you get my letters? You don't know how enervating it is not to be able to get in touch with you! That has always driven me crazy. But I'm so glad you called!'

I was touched by his excitement. 'Well, and how are you?' I answered.

'I'm fine. I mean I'm miserable! I can't function without you.'

'Well, you better learn to,' I said.

'Why?' he cried. 'Aren't you coming back?'

'Oh, I don't know. I like it here. It's hot, I got a burn just now, at the pool.'

'The pool? Aren't you working?'

Dammit, I thought, here I go. I shouldn't have called. 'The office was closed today,' I said, 'so I went over to the Montecito to sit at the pool.'

'Are you alone?'

'Perhaps I'd better hang up,' I answered.

'No please don't! I'm just being stupid. I'm so happy to hear your voice.'

'Well, I am alone,' I said. 'And I moved out of this hotel because friends of mine here, a couple, offered to put me up for a while. But he's in radio and works at night, and I can't be called there. I don't want to, I don't want to disturb him, when he sleeps.'

'Oh,' he said. 'Don't worry. I won't try to call you. Just promise to call me.'

'All right,' I said.

'When?'

'Next week.'

'When next week?'

'I'll see,' I said.

'No, you must tell me now, I might not be here.'

'I'll call next week same day, same time,' I said. 'Half past two.'

'Can't you make it two?' he asked. 'It's four hours later here, you know.'

'Good for you,' I said, 'You're going home early these days.'

'No, no,' he shouted, 'no that's not it. Half past two your time is fine. Do you promise? Do you love me?'

'I love only my cat,' I said. 'I got a cat.'

'I love cats,' he answered. 'Do you love me next best to your cat?'

I sighed.

'Please say yes,' he urged me.

'Yes.'

61

I was enveloped in care. I had thought Al would start taking me for granted after a while but he didn't, he became more and more attentive. It was clear that that man's greatest pleasure was to do things for other people – or for me, anyway. He really babied me; of course I enjoyed it although it was almost embarrassing at times. I'd say that I had a toothache and forget about it, and the following morning he had made an appointment for me with his dentist and insisted on taking me there for a check-up. We were now very often together, for he was free during the day and when I went shopping or something, he usually came along. I didn't mind that. In a paradoxical way, being in each other's company so much well-nigh neutralized our relationship. We became like a brother and sister, or better, like room-mates. With the client, whom I had loved in my fashion, we might get on each other's nerves after an hour; Al never got on my nerves. He wasn't enough 'there' for that. He was simply a sweet and unobnoxious presence. As for him – did he get out of this what he wanted? I'd guess so; he loved showing off with me everywhere (again that made me think of the client, always half-afraid of being seen with me), and he loved bringing me flowers or a magazine or something. Originally I had not worried about any sense of obligation towards him when I quit working; now I felt very much of an obligation. I was good; I kept my temper; I flirted a bit with some of his friends, just enough to keep me awake and boost his stock but I never did anything to make him jealous, never said anything to lessen him in other's eyes.

Usually we'd get up late and drive down to some restaurant for brunch around twelve. He always wanted to go in his car, which I disliked. It was closed, a waste in this climate, and moreover a Kharmann Ghia which means a camouflaged Volkswagen, a bug-like vehicle originally designed for Hitler to cart his Jerries to the wars in. 'Why don't you sell your car?' Al asked. 'It's silly for us to have two cars.'

'I need to have some things of my own,' I said, 'you mustn't try to make me totally dependent.'

He even brought me a ring with a big aquamarine which had belonged to his grandmother; I heard him having an argument about it over the telephone with his mother. I refused it, but he pleaded until I had to agree to wearing it every now and again.

After those years of struggling and dashing to offices at the most ungodly hours, to face pinching bosses with all their idiosyncrasies and lecherousnesses, here I was, pampered like a Siamese cat and with little to do except sit in the sun and look pretty. It was soothing; I gained ten pounds, got tanned all over, and for the first time in my life stopped biting my nails. I did not ever desire Al madly. I 'gave myself' as they said in old melodramas. It wasn't like with George in London, though; for I felt warm and grateful towards Al. I would have done quite a lot for him if he had asked me. I liked sleeping with him, literally sleeping, I mean. It was cosy to lie in one bed with him. But when he was in me, and pressed his body against mine, and I could feel his heart pounding madly, the situation sometimes seemed idiotic, a stupid physical performance without rhyme or reason.

62

I did not call the client back. Al and I were out that day, staying with some friends of his who had a beach house at Malibu. I thought about it as we were all eating hot dogs and clams on the beach; it wouldn't be too tricky to go into the house at half past two and place a collect call. But I disliked the idea. Here everyone was going out of his way to be nice; Al had held my hand when we were in the sea and hadn't laughed when I was scared of the high surf; now he was cooking franks and looking extremely pleased with himself and the world. Why cater to the client with his damned whims and his damned family and thus cheat on Al in a way? I didn't make up my mind about it, but when I thought of it again and asked what time it was, I had missed my hour, it was already three. Thank God, I thought, that settles it.

Some days later, at eight in the morning, I was awakened by the telephone. I got hold of it with my eyes closed; it was Jean calling me from New York.

'Jean,' I muttered, 'for God's sake, what are you up to?'

'Am I waking you?' she asked.

'Yes, you certainly are. I went to bed four hours ago.'

'Can you talk?' she asked.

Al was asleep; I took the telephone into the next room and fell in a chair. 'How did you know where I am?' I asked.

She laughed. 'I called the Montecito,' she said, 'and told them that your old office had to get in touch with you right away, matter of life and death type thing. They know our office. You must have made a hit there, they sure protect your interests.'

I sighed.

'Don't worry,' Jean said, 'I'm not going to give your number to him.'

'*Him* is the client, I guess.'

'Yes miss. He has been laying siege to me until I had to do something or I'd have gone nuts. He says he'll shoot himself if he doesn't hear from you.'

'Well, let him, to hell with him,' I said. 'How are you?'

'I'm bored. Perhaps I'll come out to Los Angeles too. It's very dreary here since you left. I have to hang up now, I'm calling you from the office. Did you promise to phone him this week?'

'Yes, I did.'

'Well, you better call him then, tell him you're off to Buenos Aires, anything; but please make this call. For me, that is.'

And so I said I would.

I came into the bedroom and looked at Al asleep there. His face was very young and carefree. I sat on the edge of his bed and started biting my nails. It was all very tiring. I went to open the kitchen door for my little cat and then went back to bed.

63

After lunch that day, I told Al I had a headache and wanted to stay alone a bit. I waited at the window till he had vanished around the curve, and then I went to the telephone. But I suddenly lost my nerve. Suppose Al should come back for something, or worse, suppose the client should trace the call? That was just the kind of thing he might do. So, cursing him, I got into my car and then saw I couldn't use the damn thing without Al's noticing it later, for he was charging the battery for me and it was hooked up to some kind of appliance.

I walked out of the house and down the hill to the nearest telephone booth; the distance was half a mile.

It was an unpleasant walk; I had never realized before how much trash, paper and beer bottles people throw along the roads here. And it was hot, and I was afraid I'd meet Al driving by.

The sun was burning on the telephone booth and I stood there with the door open, and put in my dime and spelled out the whole business to an operator who was hard of hearing. By the time I got the client on the phone, I could have killed him.

But he didn't jump on me with any 'Where have you been?' or 'Why didn't you call?'; he sounded nice, actually; calm and a bit ironic.

'Will you please stop pestering my friends?' I asked him.

He protested that he hadn't; he had just asked Jean to have me get in touch with him as I had promised anyway. Jean had been impressed with his interest in me; I shouldn't forget, he said, that it was very glamorous to be pursued across the nation by a man. Why could Jean call me if he couldn't, he asked.

'But no one can,' I said. 'I just want to be left alone! When you had me in New York, you didn't want me.'

'But I did,' he said. 'I do. Don't be a fool. You know you're not happy in that inane atmosphere. You need more than that. You're an intellectual.'

'Oh damn you. I'm not,' I said. I was almost in tears. 'Why don't you leave me alone? I was so happy here.'

He laughed fatherly. 'That's not happiness, sweetie,' he said, 'that's just a complacent cow-like life. I'm not leaving you alone because you don't want to be left alone. I'll be free. I will be divorced sometime this year. We'll get married.'

'I don't want to marry anyone, ever,' I said bitterly.

'Oh yes you do. Now you just wind up your affairs there, and come on back. I'm expecting you. I'll write you all about it. Give me an address.'

'If you promise me: no telegrams, no special delivery letters,' I said. I gave him the address of the office I had worked in. I could call the mail room and tell them.

'I love you very much,' he said, and hung up.

I trudged back up the hillside, had a shower, put my hair up, and went to the kitchen. Al was received home that day with drinks made, hors d'oeuvre, music playing, and me looking extremely spruced up. 'You're very sweet to do all that,' he said.

I felt bad.

64

Dinner at a place called The Cock and Bull, a pseudo-London pub but nice; eight of us around a table. I'm a bit high. We're all being treated by a young man (he looks eighteen) who just made thirty thousand dollars on a recording – 'For two days work, boys. Not bad.' Indeed not bad. Money, even for those who don't make it, seems always in such easy reach here, it makes life completely different. I have an image of a huge pile of everything this world has to offer, clothes, cars, houses, even trips, sun tans, health, the whole bit – and all of us feverishly loading our little or big carts from it. I know this process is supposed to be ruled by intricate economic laws, but not here, here it's just a lottery: our host is probably no better musician than the fellow next to him who borrowed twenty dollars from Al yesterday. They don't take money less seriously because of that (to the contrary), but they take not having it not seriously. That's to say, everyone presumes that he can afford everything. They are a million miles away from my former world where a dentist bill or the rent or even a pair of stockings used to be a potential problem – not to mention the world of a still lower order of human beings, people, perhaps just a couple of blocks way from The Cock and Bull, who, say, are dying right now because they can't afford a series of blood transfusions. The threat of that world, where you may die for lack of money, has been with me most of my twenty years, I think; it hasn't urged me on as the Horatio Alger fans would have it – it has scared the wits out of me. It has made me smile at bosses who were unmitigated bastards. I look at Al, who sits beside me, and I smile at him; I feel beholden, nothing less, because he has taken me out of that. There is a great sense of security in being with him.

But, I think, I'm only twenty. I shouldn't be a coward. I do not think about the damn client.

A girl at our table sings a blues that goes:

I can't eat the marriage licence,
Because I'm no nanny goat,
But I can laugh in your face
And cut your doggone throat.

65

I called the mail-room boy at the office they kicked me out of and was informed there were some letters for me. I discovered that I had hoped there wouldn't be; it would have been a relief if the client had given up.

It was a rotten dilemma; Al asked me why I looked so miserable and I couldn't even think of a soothing answer. I hated myself. I didn't go to get those letters. Why would I. I knew what they said.

After a week of this, I called the client again. I told him I wasn't sure of my plans; he ignored that. He stumbled over his words in his haste to outline all the things we were going to do once I got back. He was taking me to Europe this summer, he was looking for a bigger apartment in town, and on and on.

One morning, on the spur of the moment, I stopped as I was going by Generous Joe's Used Car Lot and drove my beautiful white convertible in there.

'Two hundred and fifty dollars,' Joe said. I told him I'd bring the car in the afternoon. I came back home with my bag of groceries, and announced to Al I was going to sell my car.

He was terribly pleased, he kissed me and said, 'You're a darling.'

Oh damn damn damn, I thought. 'Listen,' I answered, 'it's not what you think. I just want some money. And I have to send Susan the hundred dollars I still owe her.'

He didn't believe me. 'Honey,' he said, 'when you need money, you must ask me. You're my fiancée.'

'I'm nobody's fiancée,' I said. 'I'm going into a nunnery.'

66

I had to pin myself down or I'd have gone around the bend.

First, I said to myself, it is of no importance to man or beast whether some silly girl, me that is, lives in New York or in Los Angeles. So cool it, kid. Secondly, I do know New York is my town. The client is a card-carrying bastard, but he is a grown-up. I respect him, he is stronger than I am. Al is sweet and weak; it isn't even fair to him to live with him like this and use him as a refuge. His mother will find some nice Jewish un-neurotic girl for him and they'll marry and have four children. I'm not leading the right kind of life for me.

I sent a telegram to the client which said that I'd be back in New York in two weeks, that I had a bad cold and couldn't leave sooner.

I thus started on my period of low cunning, as I called it for myself. I bought a ticket to New York on Transcontinental Airlines for Saturday 15 May. They're the cheapest. The man asked me my address and I caught myself just in time and said I had no fixed address but was travelling around. I bought a cat basket. I took my clothes to the cleaners. One day as we passed a radio cab, I noticed its telephone number and memorized it. I was nice to Al.

I told him not to call me his fiancée, but I didn't dare say more than that.

That was really all there was to it, outwardly. But underneath, those two weeks were very bad. Nothing we said or did had the same meaning for Al as for me. He often talked about the future; he loved making plans, he was going to look for a house with a swimming pool, he was going to give a big party. And even the most innocuous remarks of his had a terrible edge to them for me now. I knew I wouldn't be there when the man would come for the newspaper money. I knew I wouldn't be there on his birthday. I knew I wouldn't be there for that dinner invitation he accepted for both of us. I was doing it myself: but this discovery, that you can live at the side of another person, eat and sleep with him, feel his seed enter into the deepest of your body, and yet so easily maintain secrecy, dissimulation of your thoughts, was very frightening. It had a crime-like colour; I was only planning to leave a man whom I had never promised anything and it felt as if I were planning his murder – the web of little lies was the same. I had never before had the idea that there is something so specific about fraud, about cheating, something so ungradual.

67

I must have looked green that last Saturday, because Al said, 'You're not coming to the studio with me, you're staying home. Go to bed early.' I nodded. I was so miserable. I had told myself that if he'd insist on my coming to the studio with him I'd go and forget the whole plot. But that was probably a lie to myself.

When he had left, I phoned New York. It didn't matter any more now if the call was traced, but I called collect of course; right while I was doing this, I hated the client, he should pay, for this call, for everything Al had ever bought me. When the client answered the telephone, I couldn't speak. I started to cry. 'What is it?' he asked. 'What's the matter with you?'

'I don't know,' I finally managed to say, 'I'm just shook up. I hate leaving here.'

'Well –,' he said.

'Are you sure you want me? Are you sure you want me to come back? Won't we have the same scenes again?'

'Now listen calmly, girl,' the client said. 'If I weren't sure, I wouldn't have written. You were gone. You had completely vanished from my life. I've had almost two months without you. If I didn't love you, I'd be over it by now. I'd tell you even now, "Just stay where you are".'

'Yes, you should.'

'But I do love you. You must trust me. You know you love me, you know you want to come back – don't you?'

'Yes,' I mumbled. 'But – I just don't have the strength to pack, and get to the airport.'

'Can't your friends help you?' he asked rather sharply.

'No, they're away.'

'Well, I can't come out there to do it for you. Come on now, pull yourself together and get a move on.'

'All right, I will,' I said. 'My plane leaves at eleven. I'll call you when I'm in New York.'

I took my suitcase down and threw everything I owned into it. Then I sat down and wrote a letter to Al. I said that I didn't love him and that it wasn't fair to use him this way, and stop him from finding a girl who would marry him, which was what he wanted and needed. I said I longed for New York, which was my home. I said he was the dearest man I had ever met, and would he please, please forgive me. I took off the ring and put it with the letter on the table.

Then I telephoned for a taxi and went into the garden to get my cat. Until then she'd always come running when I called her, and this night she hid. I finally saw her eyes gleam under a bush and dragged her out and put her in her basket, with the tears streaming down my face. I took my suitcase and my gramophone – I had to search for it, Al had a stereo set and he had stored it away – and the cat basket, carried them out one by one and locked the door.

I walked down the path to the gate, and waited for the cab to the airport.

68

'Oh my God,' the client said as he carried my suitcase and my basket up the stairs to his place, 'a cat!'

'I told you.'

'I know. But where are we going to put it? I'm such a light sleeper.'

'It's a she,' I said.

We sat down on his bed and looked at each other.

'Do you live here now?' I asked.

'Yes, she has the house on the Island. We're officially separated.'

'It's a tiny place.'

'I know. Don't worry. I promised you, didn't I? I'll go apartment hunting, as soon as I have the time.'

'Are you glad to see me?' I asked.

'You look terrible,' he said with a laugh. 'Obviously New York agrees with you more than Los Angeles. But yes, I'm glad to see you.' He pulled me towards him and kissed me.

'I need a shower,' I said, 'it was a tiresome flight. Everybody was throwing up.' I opened Gyor's basket and she came out hesitantly. 'Go say hello to your master,' I told her and put her in the client's lap.

I took my toilet bag out of my suitcase and went into his bathroom. I wasn't thinking much; it will all fall into place, I told myself. Al's just a kid, he'll go see his friends, get very drunk, and then he'll be over it.

I came out. I was naked and smiled at the client and lay down on the bed. It was the best way to handle it, I thought. He looked at me, stood up and took off his clothes, and lay beside me.

'Well?' I said.

He put my hand on his sex, and I caressed him until he could come into me. He only moved a few times, and then he came, clutching me very hard. 'I'm sorry to be so quick,' he murmured. And I didn't think of him at all, I saw the house in the Hollywood Hills, and Al sitting in his kitchen, and again I started to cry. Oh dammit, I told myself, this has got to stop, this is the last time.

'What is it?' he asked. 'Are you homesick for Los Angeles?'

I shook my head and swallowed. 'I'll be all right,' I said, 'I just have to get used to things again – all these changes – just give me a day or so.' And I went to the bathroom to blow my nose.

69

I didn't quite feel up to calling my mother yet but the client made me do it. My stepfather answered the telephone and he told me, sounding peeved more than anything else, that she was very sick. 'Why didn't you warn me?' I asked, and he said she had written me a letter to that hotel in Los Angeles and it had been returned. And so that same Sunday afternoon I got on another plane and flew to Watertown. I had wanted to wait till Monday morning, but the client said I might as well go right away; it was better, and it would give him a chance to do some things and buy a wider bed on Monday. I decided to keep my fingers crossed for my mother without ever letting go during the whole flight and I managed to.

There was no one at the airport in Watertown and after I had waited awhile I found a cab willing to take me to my parents' house. When I rang the bell, my stepfather opened the door as quickly as if he had been waiting behind it. He looked at me without stepping aside and then he said, 'Your mother is dead.'

She had died at eight o'clock that evening, two hours before I got to her.

That visit in the hospital room in New York was the last time I ever spoke to her; and before that, Christmas when she bought me the gloves; and before that, the mute dinner at the Croydon hotel; and before that, nothing really: a haphazard exchange of functional sentences through my childhood. She was my mother. Now it was over.

I went to see her; she looked thin and tired. I didn't cry.

I stayed until the funeral, which was Tuesday. When we came back to the house, my stepfather told me I could have some of her things if I wanted them as keepsakes, but he trailed me through the rooms as if afraid I'd put the silver in my pockets. I took only some old photographs of her and me. Then I thought of shipping back my locker to New York, but he informed me he had refused delivery: 'You're a grown woman now,' he said, 'you must understand you can't saddle other people with your problems.' He didn't know what the Express men had done with it. 'Do you want to pay something towards the funeral?' he asked, and I said I'd mail him a cheque from New York. The neighbour's gardener, who had come over to help, drove me back to the airport.

Of the photographs I have, in the one I like best, I'm sitting on a fence. My mother stands near me but she isn't looking at me. There's nothing written on the back; I think I'm seven or eight in it, and I don't look so very different from the way I look now. I'm wearing a little hat, and some kind of navy blouse, a skirt and knee socks; I'm a pretty girl, with long hair. My mother is smiling, she's quite handsome. She wears a hat too.

It's a big garden we're in, or maybe a pasture. It is a sunny picture.

70

Someone once told me that New York is the capital of the western world. I like that idea. If I were a communist or from the eastern half of the earth or something, I guess I'd want to live in Moscow; but since I'm not, I want to live in New York. There's nothing else; the other places, even London, are provincial, also-rans, in comparison.

It was soothing to be back and to walk again on real streets and look at the people of New York.

I treated Jean to lunch and told her my story, and she said she thought I had done right. I informed her that one shouldn't live in a vacuum, that you had to be able to show something for your days rolling by. I needed a man like the client who wanted you to think; I was going to study things, French to begin with, I was going to bother. That was the kind of life I was going to lead.

I told her about my mother.

'Are you very sad?' Jean muttered.

'I'm glad I'm with him,' I said, 'or I'd feel sort of rudderless. Not that she ... I'm sad for her. Her life must have seemed pointless to her, in the end, perhaps – they were so, so self-centred, these two.'

Jean shrugged. 'Who isn't,' she answered.

That evening, lying in the new bed with the client, I talked about my luncheon with Jean. 'She's a nice girl,' he said, 'I don't think she approves of me though.'

'Oh yes, she thinks you're terrific. Very handsome.' Then, after a while, I remarked, 'Jean told me that my old job is open. My successor didn't last.'

He looked at me. 'What did you say to that?' he asked.

'Nothing. Should I have said something?'

He hesitated. 'Well, no, I just wondered.'

'Would you like me to try and get it back?' I insisted.

'Oh, I just thought,' he said, 'this place is so cramped – to sit around in – and heaven knows we're not too flush, I had a lot of expenses.'

'But if we go to Europe this summer, how could I take it?' I asked.

'Yes, of course, that would be a problem.'

'Are you sorry you made me come back?' I asked him.

'No, of course not! Are you sorry you came back?'

'No. I'm never sorry about anything I do.'

'I know you were having a marvellous time out there,' he suddenly said.

'What do you mean by that?'

'Nothing.'

I waited for him to say more, but he didn't. We turned away from each other; I fell asleep.

71

The client took me to a Schubert concert one evening. It was soothing; I enjoyed it.

When we were set to go home, his car wouldn't start.

He swore, jumped out, looked under the hood, and rummaged in the trunk for his flashlight. 'Damn it all,' he said, 'this one evening, wouldn't you believe it, I left the flashlight at home.' He looked furious. 'Cars don't bring out the best in you,' I said, thinking of our first flat tyre in Miami.

'What the hell do you mean by that?' he asked.

'I don't mean anything.'

He said he was going to get a mechanic from somewhere and walked away. Before he had reached the corner, two young men stopped by me and asked could they help. I saw that the client had turned around and was watching me. I didn't know what he wanted me to do; I thought I might save him the chasing for a garage. So I said, 'Well, if you know about engines, please have a look.'

As one of the men peered under the hood, and the other offered me a cigarette which I refused because I do not smoke, the client reappeared on the scene. He tapped the mechanically minded fellow on his shoulder and said, 'Don't bother, we'll manage.'

The two men looked at him and walked away.

'Why – ' I began but he interrupted me.

'What the hell do you think you're doing,' he muttered at me through clenched teeth. 'Are you crazy, letting strangers talk to you? I don't care if you're a pickup, but not when you're with me, see?'

I stared at him.

'Look at that dress,' he said. 'This is not California, you know. You look like a whore.'

I looked at my dress, a very gay yellow summer dress with shoestring shoulder straps.

The client closed his eyes, and wiped his forehead.

I opened the car door, took my pocketbook from the front seat, and wanted to walk away. He held me by the arm, and I shook loose. 'I'm sorry, I'm sorry!' he almost shouted, 'don't leave me here like this.' People turned around at us. I said, 'You won't see me again. Nobody calls me a pickup. You must have gone out of your mind. But that's your business, I'll leave you to it.'

'Don't be so high and mighty,' he said bitterly. 'Weren't you picked up by that guy in Los Angeles?'

I was so startled that I stood still. 'Weren't you?' he said. 'Weren't you? By that Al, or whatever his name is?'

I reddened.

'You thought I didn't know, didn't you,' he went on. 'Well, I did. I knew after a week. I've friends there too. Don't forget it was me who sent you to the Montecito Hotel, kid.'

'Then why did you make me come back?' I asked slowly.

He took a deep breath. He shrugged. 'Because I want you back,' he said.

'Why didn't you speak up when I phoned you?' I asked.

'There'd have been a big scene – it's not something to straighten out on the phone. It would have cost a fortune in calls back and forth. If I had said I knew, you wouldn't have come back, you'd have thought I would be jealous –'

I didn't know what to say; I just stared at him.

'I'm not jealous,' he said. 'I was upset when I heard, not jealous – oh, I'm sorry. I apologize. It's just that when I saw you talking to these men, I felt –'

I was so tired at that instant that if I hadn't sat down I'd have fallen on the pavement. I got back into the car and sat still, clutching my pocketbook. The client looked at me, hesitated, and walked off to get his mechanic.

72

She didn't have the courage to admit to herself that she might have made such a mistake, and so she ignored that incident. She got up mornings with him, and after he'd left, she would scrub and clean the place, and then read the paper. She'd mark apartment ads which looked promising and go and look at them later. She had long conversations with Jean on the telephone. She washed her hair. She sat at the window in his one good chair, and read his books. She talked to her cat. She waited.

When he came home, she jumped up and put her arms around his neck, and he would kiss her and look happy to find her there. 'I'm spending my days here like an old lady with her cat,' she told him. She'd report to him about the apartments and he'd react with half-sentences like, 'Yes we should –' or 'I'll look into it as soon as –' He told her he had only two hundred dollars left in his account, but she shrugged and didn't ask him how they were supposed to go to Europe on that. He didn't mention divorce or marriage. She felt a great resentment, fury almost, hidden underneath his pleasantness, and she chose not to touch it, she didn't question what he did or planned to do. They both pretended to be living from day to day. She was now spending her last dollars, but she didn't ask him for money, and he didn't bring it up. There was no lustre to making love with him then, but he was desperately eager. She became unwell and although that usually didn't bother her, this time she couldn't make love; she'd bring a towel to bed and pet him. She didn't mind, but he would afterwards go on about being sorry and feeling too greedy, and did she really not hate him for it – until she said, 'If you ask me once more, I *will* hate you for it.'

There came a summery evening; she had made a salad for them for dinner, she had cleaned up afterwards, and was now sitting on the bed, reading a magazine of his; he was behind his desk typing a letter. The article was of a kind she had never tried to read before, it was very involved. She had thought it would be a great bore, but now it fascinated her. For she liked the idea of both of them working at something, thinking about different things, but in the same room.

There was a warm light in the street outside, a haze rising from the trees.

She had the feeling then that it would turn out right after all; that he was serious about them; that he now had swallowed his jealousies; and that they'd have a new start. She had a quick, intense sensation of oneness with him; she went over to him and put many little kisses on his face. But it remained a closed face. She stepped back and sat in the window sill.

'Why do you look at me that way?' he asked.

She didn't answer.

'Christ, I'm bored,' he suddenly burst out. 'I'm going to mail a letter.' And he left the room.

A little later she went out into the street too and walked up Lexington Avenue. On the second corner she came to a telephone booth. She went in and placed a call to Al. She let it ring four times; there was no answer. Then she lost her nerve and hung up.

73

When I told Jean about my trying to telephone Al, she stared at me aghast. 'Are you crazy,' she said. 'What would you have told the poor bastard? He's just recovered by now, and you're going to stir it all up again. *Why*?'

'Because I didn't know what else to do.'

'Oh for Chrissake,' she said. 'Look honey, it's one thing to walk out on a man, everybody is doing it, we on them, they on us. All's fair, et cetera. But you can't fall back on them when you're having trouble with the Love of your Life.'

I smiled wanly.

'Well, that's what he is, no, the client I mean?'

'Yes.'

'Well, next time you just call *me* collect. I'll open a Client Anonymous.'

I told Jean then that the client had known about Al, and that once he had broken that up, he had changed completely, and had become like an enemy. That's what he had wanted to accomplish, I thought.

'Did you know he called me yesterday to find out were you happy with him, and happy in New York?' Jean asked.

That surprised me greatly.

'Well, you see,' she said, 'there's more to it. You should have seen the state he was in when you were gone. You're living with him – don't sneeze at that. This is a cruel city, you know. When I left Stamford,' she added, 'my father told me, in New York, when you're in danger, you must cry "fire!" and all your neighbours will come running. If you cry "help", they'll lock their doors and turn up their TV's.'

That scared me. I looked at her. She was really sweet, I thought, to go on listening to my crap. 'I'm not in danger,' I said, 'but turn up your TV anyway.'

74

It was lovely weather that weekend, but everything else was rotten.

The client was morose; on Sunday we went to Jones Beach with friends of his and he behaved terribly. At one point one of them spread out a beach towel and said, not even very seriously, something like, 'You sit here with your fiancée,' and he answered, 'What fiancée? I have no fiancée. This girl is my telephone pal,' and they all looked at how I'd react. When I said, 'Come in the water with me,' he made a face and answered, 'No, you go right ahead. I don't want to cramp your style with all those handsome lifeguards.'

The meanest thing was when we were sitting in the back seat of their car on the way home and I asked him again, softly, '*Why* did you make me come back to New York?' and he answered in a loud voice, 'Come on. You wanted to come back anyway – no man can make you do something you don't want to do.' 'Oh, screw you Jack,' I said to that, and they laughed.

He wanted to make love to me all the same that night, but I told him I was sore there. He tossed around for an hour, to demonstrate his frustration, I guess.

'Don't ask me any more *why's*,' he suddenly said loudly. 'Because I won't forgive you, that's why.'

'Forgive me for what?'

'For cheating on me,' he said.

'Do you want me to leave?'

'Do what you want. You do, anyway.'

I got dressed and walked around the block what seemed a million times. But I couldn't even think very much. When I'm in a mess, I can never muster my thoughts; they just flutter around somewhere up high, and I'm left to wander alone down below and resort to the counting of steps of staircases, crossing pavements without stepping on cracks, or trying to hold my breath until a traffic light changes.

75

I woke up in the night, it was dark and silent in the room but I felt that he was awake.

'What is it?' I whispered.

'I don't know,' the client said, 'I just can't sleep, I feel scared or something.'

'Of what?'

'I don't know. Of myself. Of life.'

So I took his head on my shoulder.

'Sing something for me,' he asked.

And I sang, '– la la la art, la la in darkest hour, when in the mm mm coils of life enmeshed –'

He listened very quietly. 'That was lovely,' he finally said. 'What is it?'

'"To Music." Schubert.'

'Well, fancy that,' he said, 'I didn't know you knew things like that . . . Please sing it again.'

It was almost like our very beginning. But not really.

76

I had promised myself not to burst into tears any more and stuck to that. I did cry once more when I talked again to Al, but I'm afraid that was a bit of an act: I had called him one time without getting him but tried again some days later, no matter what Jean had said; and when he answered the phone he caught me so unprepared for any speech I had no way out but crying.

That was very good. He talked, and I just made indefinable sounds in between.

He said, of course he had forgiven me. He understood quite well, I was a young girl and his seriousness and wanting to get married had scared me. I wanted to have fun; but we can have fun together, he said, running around with different men and playing the field isn't really fun, it leaves you with a terrible taste in your mouth. All that stuff grows stale very fast. And I shouldn't waste my years in some crummy office either. It had been a blow to come home and find my letter and the ring. But he knew that wasn't the end of it.

'I – ,' I said.

'Will you marry me?' he asked.

I said something that sounded like, 'Oh.'

'I want you to come back,' he said, 'but not just to stay with me. That's no good any more. I want to marry you.'

'You're sweet,' I murmured.

'I'm going to buy a ticket for you today,' he announced. 'It'll be waiting for you at the American Airlines place in New York. It should be there by the end of this week. Or don't you want that?'

Silence on my part.

'All right then,' he said, 'You'll see. All's well that ends well. I'll make you happy.'

'I don't know – ,' I said.

'I'll send a ticket, anyway. I'll know for both of us.'

On Friday morning I walked to the airline ticket office and, indeed, there was a prepaid ticket in my name.

77

She felt a different girl, carrying around a plane ticket in her pocketbook. It was her armour.

Obviously it wasn't fair to Al to use it this way, she thought. But she wouldn't for long. Say, at most five days. Five days was not an extravagant term.

And she told herself, if you really want something, surely you've got a good chance to manage it – like winning the client around. After all, another woman had got him once.

In the meantime, she walked. Their apartment was only five blocks from her old office, and she walked there to visit Jean, and to her old stores to try on things. She had just a few dollars left but now she didn't mind. She went to the library and to the French Institute to see about its classes, and to the New School. She typed up a list of possibilities.

The weather was radiant, with a hot sun and cool prisms of shadow along the house blocks.

She still had some of her Montecito tan, and she looked at herself in the mirrors in shop windows and was pleased.

Young New York matron – she had seen that somewhere in a caption in a magazine. It sounded sort of awful, she thought, but she liked it all the same. She felt a bit like that, then.

78

The client said he had an evening engagment, and I went over to Jean's for dinner. I brought her a pound of hamburger from his refrigerator.

'You look a hell of a lot better,' Jean said.

'I've got a plane ticket,' I told her.

'Damn you,' she said. And that if I didn't know what I wanted, I shouldn't do anything, but quietly start from scratch, borrow some money (not from her, she was broke), take a room at the Y and look for a job. I agreed.

We talked about California. She wanted to have a go at it too, she thought.

It was about eleven when I came home, and as I put my key in the lock I could see the light under the door. I was very happy he was home. I opened the door and greeted him with a big fat smile.

Then I saw that his face was pale and drawn, and he said in a strange, choked voice, 'Sit down, I have to talk to you.'

I felt as if he'd hit me in my stomach. Oh God, I thought, now what.

I closed the door and sat in the easy chair. 'What is it?' I muttered.

'I found this,' he said. 'Would you care to explain it?' And he handed me the plane ticket.

I looked at it and then I started to smile, idiotically. I don't know why, I couldn't stop myself. Heaven knows I didn't think there was anything funny.

The client lifted his arm as if he were going to slap me. 'Don't smile that way,' he screamed. 'I've seen you look that way before. You're a tramp.'

I stood up.

'And where had you planned to fly to?' he asked. 'Back to mister Al?'

I went over to the closet and pulled out my suitcase.

'What do you think you're doing?' he shouted.

'I'm leaving right now,' I said. 'There's really no point in screaming at each other all night.' I put the suitcase on the bed and began to pack quickly.

He sat down and observed me awhile. Then he said, 'Don't go now. Please don't. Wait till tomorrow. Let's talk this over.'

'There's nothing to talk about, you don't want me, and you don't want anyone else to have me,' I said. 'And I don't want to live with a man who goes through my pocketbook when I'm not there.'

'Please stay,' he repeated. 'Just to sleep. I don't want to make love either.'

When I had packed, I got my basket down from the shelf in the kitchenette and locked Gyor in it.

The client stood up and said, 'Don't leave me here alone in the middle of the night.' He was shivering now as if he had a fever. 'Leave your cat with me at least,' he then asked.

'I need my cat.'

I put my suitcase in the outside corridor, came back for Gyor and my coat, and left the apartment. I didn't take the gramophone, I couldn't carry it.

He came out after me; I didn't go fast with my luggage and he stayed a few steps behind me on the staircase.

I walked into the middle of the street; an empty cab turned into our block from the avenue and I stopped it. The client stood beside me now; he didn't speak or move. Then, when my things were in, he suddenly sprinted off. I saw him unlock his own car which was parked near the end of the street, across from the apartment.

I got into the cab, bent over and told the chauffeur, 'Listen to me. You must not drive ahead. Back up the street and go down Lexington.' I was pretty near the end of my tether at that point, and the driver must have seen it on my face, for he didn't say a word and just did as I had asked. When we were past the first light on the avenue, I sat back and asked, 'To Idlewild, please.'

'Kennedy,' the driver answered and gave me a little nod in the mirror.

We got there at quarter to two in the morning. When I had paid him, I had seventy-five cents left. I carried my things in and sat down in a metal chair opposite the American Airlines counter. At any rate I was in no rush; the first plane out was posted for nine forty-five.

I went into a phone booth to call Al, but I couldn't quite make it. I sent a collect telegram.

There was no one in the hall.

A *Daily News* was lying on a chair near me. I took some of the inner pages and put them under Gyor in her basket, and started reading the remaining ones.

The metallic light in that empty space softened. Day was breaking. I stepped outside. The sky was overcast, it had rained before dawn. The air was very fresh and tasted almost wet.

79

When I was a child, once during the summer I was farmed out to a market gardener's family living in a cottage somewhere in Surrey. They had a girl my age. At the end of the summer, a note came from my mother to send me back, and in the morning they put me on a big green, rural bus to Woldingham.

I had forgotten all about that time. And then on my plane going west, I dreamt of it and remembered it all in my dream. When I opened my eyes, I thought for one second I was on that bus.

We flew over the clouds until we had crossed the Rocky Mountains, where suddenly the earth became visible through white shreds of fog. I thought I could even see the thin lines of the highways, along which Susan and I had crawled for so many days, three months ago.

And then they were already thanking us for flying with them and telling us not to smoke until we were in the terminal. I had one single moment of panic and thought of hiding in the plane until Al was out of sight, and going off somewhere alone, managing somehow. But it passed.

As soon as I got through the door, I saw him waving at me; he was standing outside the entrance gate to the terminal. I smiled at him, and when I got there, I put my arms around him.

The first thing I said was, 'You're not supposed to take a cat in the cabin with you. But I did and she didn't make a sound.'

And he, 'I got a parking spot quite near by.'

80

Al has never questioned me on my running off to New York, never asked if I had a boy friend there, and never made a crack about my lies those last two weeks before I left. Perhaps we should have had a big fat scene about it; but we didn't.

When we got to the house, he put the ring back on my hand and announced, 'Next week we're getting married.' Then he carried my things into his bedroom and said, 'Go to bed. You look pooped. I'll wake you at six and we'll eat something on the way to the radio station.'

Al took me along to look for houses for rent; he said we needed a bigger place and he wanted a pool. The real-estate agent who drove us around called me 'the little lady'. I sat in the back and when we got to a place, he'd jump out, open the door for me and cry, 'Let's see whether the little lady likes this one!' It was tiring.

But I realize he was just making a living, muddling through like all of us.

Al was so sure I was thrilled by this expedition that I acted thrilled, I had to. He took a house which wasn't quite ready yet; they were still painting and putting in wires. We went to look at it every day and he brought a camera along and photographed me on the steps. The real-estate man took a picture of us two, Al with his arm around my middle. The pictures all came out well.

Al got three days off and we drove to Tijuana to get married. A friend of his promised to come and feed Gyor while we were away. It was the first time I was down in Mexico, but it's so close to the border there that you hear more English than Spanish. I gather we went to Mexico because Al's mother was fighting the marriage; I heard them shout at each other over the telephone, but I stayed out of it. Al had taken me over once to see her, but that visit had not been a great success. She didn't want her son to marry a gentile. When we drove home, he had announced he'd never speak to her again. 'Don't be silly,' I said.

In Tijuana we went to a lawyer; his office was in his home, right in the living room. We sat on a stuffed couch and Al signed papers while children ran in and out of the room, and the telephone rang every few minutes. Then we went to see a judge. I had no time to get nervous. I signed a form, and the judge said, 'Congratulations. You are now man and wife.'

They hadn't even asked to see my driver's licence or anything; it was easier than paying with a cheque at Bloomingdale's.

That night, for the first time, after Al had made love to me, he propped himself up on his elbow, looked me in my face and asked, 'Did you – did you come too?'

'Yes,' I said softly.

81

And so, like a fairy tale, this story of mine ends where I got married and am living in a gorgeous house with a garden and a swimming pool. I'm not being cynical about it either.

Al is a nice man. One evening after his programme, someone said something about him joining a little band (he plays the piano), and he immediately answered, 'Me, never. We can't live on that kind of money.' And I know he doesn't like Gyor, but he never says a word about it because I love her.

As far as my *revolución* is concerned, it has to get on without me, which is no loss on either side. Every day that goes by, the world is in a bigger mess anyway and what they tell us about it is mostly phoney, or that's how it seems to me.

So you might just as well concentrate on yourself. Nipso ipso, or whatever the client's Greek proverb said.

I do think about him and wonder what became of him.

But not too much.

As the song says, bless 'em all.

More about Penguins and Pelicans

Penguinews, which appears every month, contains details of all the new books issued by Penguins as they are published. From time to time it is supplemented by *Penguins in Print*, which is a complete list of all available books published by Penguins (There are well over four thousand of these.)

A specimen copy of *Penguinews* will be sent to you free on request. For a year's issues (including the complete lists) please send 50p if you live in the United Kingdom, or 75p if you live elsewhere. Just write to Dept EP, Penguin Books Ltd, Harmondsworth, Middlesex, enclosing a cheque or postal order, and your name will be added to the mailing list.

Note: *Penguinews* and *Penguins in Print* are not available in the U.S.A. or Canada

Charles Webb

The Graduate

'For twenty-one years I have been shuffling back and forth between classrooms and libraries. Now you tell me what the hell it's got me.'

That's how Benjamin Braddock talked when he came down from university. Somehow it didn't seem to be what his father expected from a college education. And everyone was really appalled when Ben raped Mrs Robinson (that was her story anyway) and ran off with her daughter in the middle of her wedding to someone else . . .

A brilliantly sordid tale of a young man's search for identity and a portrayal of the worst-behaved yet most sympathetic anti-hero of the day.

Not for sale in the U.S.A. or Canada

Charles Webb

The Marriage of a Young Stockbroker

The Marriage of a Young Stockbroker is much like other young American marriages. After eighteen months of it, Lisa leaves Bill during their summer holiday by the sea. Not that both parties wouldn't like to make their marriage work according to the ideal American formula. But what is that formula? If they could only discover why they got together in the first place, they might make a start, though Lisa's sister, Nan, would be determined to foil them...